Duffle Bag Cartel 4

Lock Down Publications and Ca$h
Presents
Duffle Bag Cartel 4
A Novel by *Ghost*

Lock Down Publications
P.O. Box 870494
Mesquite, Tx 75187

Visit our website @
www.lockdownpublications.com

Copyright 2020 by Ghost
Duffle Bag Cartel 4

First Edition April 2020
Printed in the United States of America

This is a work of fiction. Names, characters, places, and incidents either are products of the author's imagination or are used fictitiously. Any similarity to actual events or locales or persons, living or dead, is entirely coincidental.

Lock Down Publications
Like our page on Facebook: Lock Down Publications @
www.facebook.com/lockdownpublications.ldp
Cover design and layout by: **Dynasty Cover Me**
Book interior design by: **Shawn Walker**
Edited by: **Mia Rucker**

Stay Connected with Us!

Text **LOCKDOWN** to 22828 to stay up-to-date with new releases, sneak peaks, contests and more…

Thank you.

Submission Guideline.

Submit the first three chapters of your completed manuscript to ldpsubmissions@gmail.com, subject line: Your book's title. The manuscript must be in a .doc file and sent as an attachment. Document should be in Times New Roman, double spaced and in size 12 font. Also, provide your synopsis and full contact information. If sending multiple submissions, they must each be in a separate email.

Have a story but no way to send it electronically? You can still submit to LDP/Ca$h Presents. Send in the first three chapters, written or typed, of your completed manuscript to:

LDP: Submissions Dept
Po Box 870494
Mesquite, Tx 75187

DO NOT send original manuscript. Must be a duplicate.

Provide your synopsis and a cover letter containing your full contact information.

Thanks for considering LDP and Ca$h Presents.

Dedications:

First of all, this book is dedicated to my Baby Girl 3/10, the love of my life and purpose for everything I do. As long as I'm alive, you'll never want nor NEED for anything. We done went from flipping birds to flipping books. The best is yet to come.

To LDP'S CEO- Ca$h & COO- Shawn:

I would like to thank y'all for this opportunity. The wisdom, motivation, and encouragement that I've received from you two is greatly appreciated.

The grind is real. The loyalty in this family is real. I'm riding with LDP 'til the wheels fall off.

THE GAME IS OURS !

I GOT THE STREETS!

Ghost

Chapter 1

Smoke took two steps back and aimed his pistol at Phoenix. He slid his thumbs down the hammers and cocked them. He curled his lip. "Cuz, I cut that bitch up at Mikey's request, and that ain't all," he snickered. "Yo, Mikey, come on out, big homie. Let's stop playing games with this nigga."

Phoenix took two steps back as Mikey stepped into the room with a bound Natalia. He threw her at Phoenix's feet and kicked her as hard as he could in her back. She screamed in pain and rolled on to her side. Both of her eyes were blackened.

Mikey held a Forty Glock in his right hand. "Yo bitch got a five million dollar bounty on her head. Whew. That was too much money to pass up, even for Smoke. They say that revenge is a dish best served cold, Phoenix. I'm about to test that theory. Smoke, tie this nigga up. We're about to have some fun. After his torturous death, I am officially announcing my leadership of the Duffle Bag Cartel." Mikey looked over to Phoenix and laughed. "Yeah, I like the sound of that."

Smoke mugged Phoenix for what felt like a long time. Then he stepped backward shaking his head. "Nall, fuck that. That shit doesn't make sense to me either. Both of you niggas got me fucked up." Smoke spit on the concrete. He nodded his head real hard, geeking himself up. Then he pointed a gun at Mikey, and kept the other Glock pinned on Phoenix.

Phoenix smiled. "Now I'm wit that shit, nigga. If you gon blow my shit back, then do it, but you make sho you knock his top off, too. I always had your best interest at heart. This fuck nigga, Mikey, ain't been about shit but his self. So fuck him."

Mikey aimed his gun at Smoke. "Fuck is you doing, mane? I thought we already had dis shit mapped out."

"N'all, Playboy, you see I'm tired of following behind you fuck niggas, period. I'm my own man, and I wanna be my own boss. You talking 'bout you finna be the new head. That just sounds like a whole lot more following to me. It's time for a mafucka to cut out the middle man. I'm ready to get a hundred percent of the street's profits instead of just a percentage of what either one of you bitch niggas giving me. So the way I see it, I'm announcing myself as head of the Duffle Bag Cartel, and you best believe that the Mound gon' follow me. I have been here since I was a youngin'. I'm from the mud. Mikey, you originally from White Haven, and Phoenix, you were born in Arizona. Ain't nan one of you niggas cut from Orange Mound. This is my shit."

"Smoke," Natalia groaned, "if you let me and Phoenix go, that five million that the Russians have on my head, I will give it to you in cash. Not to mention, I will see to it that both Phoenix and myself forgo this transgression. I understand that you just want to be your own boss. I'll plug you in around the States. That's my word."

Phoenix eyed Smoke with hatred. He couldn't believe that his lil' Homie was flipping the script on him in the manner that he was. But as much as he hated to admit it, he understood. He was prepared to fuck Smoke over if the opportunity presented itself. He didn't give a fuck what Natalia was talking about.

Smoke imagined five million dollars in cash, and he knew what he could already do with it. Tennessee was on fire because of him and Phoenix. He needed to get out of the State quickly, but he had no idea where he would go. Five million dollars would definitely help him figure it out. He took his gun off of Phoenix and aimed it at Natalia. "Bitch, are you playing with me?"

"I'm in pain, Smoke. I'm worried about the state of my unborn child. I don't have room to play with you. The money is yours. Now please just trust me." Natalia sat up, and cupped her stomach.

"You gon' trust this turncoat ass bitch? She got the Russians and all kinds of underworld mafuckas looking for her. This bitch might be dead before you even get the chance to get your money," Mikey cut in. He saw himself on the losing end of the negotiations, and he needed to make some sort of ground fast. "I got a half million right now in my trunk saying you smoke Phoenix bitch ass, and we'll deliver his bitch to the Russians ourselves. Out of the five million that they are offering for her, you can keep four, all I want is one."

"They'll kill you guys after you hand me over. Russians do not leave any loose ends, and they hate blacks the most amongst all other races outside of their own. You hand me to them, and a bullet will go through your head seconds later. I can guarantee you this." Natalia held her ribs, and winced in agony. "Smoke you know that I have a safe house. You can get your money tonight. All I ask is that you let me and Phoenix go our separate ways. We've never done anything to hurt you, or disrespected you in any way."

"Shid, look at his face. Nigga, Phoenix done already beat yo ass black and blue. You finna trust his bitch ass over me? Really?" Mikey looked to see if his comments hit Smoke at all. He was thirsty to find a mental chink in Smoke's armor.

"That was mutual combat, pussy ass nigga. And I fucked him up, too. It wasn't sweet. Plus, I ain't never been a scuffler. That's why I keep this stick on me, like I play hockey." He aimed his gun at Mikey. "You finna give me that five hundred thousand out of your trunk, and y'all finna give me that five million that shorty flexing about. I'ma take that cash and build up the Duffle Bag Cartel. I'ma be the head. Mikey, you are no longer a part of this mob, and Phoenix, neither are you. I am officially the king. Both of you niggas got that?"

Mikey scrunched his face. He was tired of playing pussy. He stepped toward Smoke, heated. "You think cause you got that gun pointed at me that I'm a bitch or something? Nigga, fuck you. You ain't runnin' shit. I'm the head. I am officially the king of the Duffle Bag Cartel and ain't shit neither of you mafuckas can do about..."

Boom. Boom. Boom.

Phoenix popped Mikey three times in the back. Mikey shook in the air, fell down to his knees, and landed on his chest. Smoke emitted from the holes in his back. Phoenix turned him over. Mikey was shaking as if he were freezing cold. "Bitch ass nigga, how it feel? Huh? How it feel to get popped by a nigga you been rolling with since before you had a moustache? Huh?" *Boom.* Another shot to the chest lifted Mikey's back from the ground, before it settled again.

Mikey's eyes fluttered, and then they closed. He was thankful that he'd worn a bulletproof vest. He only hoped that Phoenix would leave him for dead. His injuries at the moment were serious at best.

Phoenix held the gun at his side. Smoke had both of his guns trained on Phoenix. Phoenix held one hand at shoulder level. "Nigga, I ain't got shit against you, mane. You wanna lead the cartel, it's yours. I'm stepping down. That five million that my shawty talking is yours, too. Just let us leave this bitch wit' our lives, bruh."

Smoke was caught between a rock and a hard place. He looked down at Mikey and saw the smoke still coming from the gunshot wounds in his chest. He was dead. Smoke was sure of it. He bent down and took Mikey's car keys off of him. "Look, mane, I ain't kill Alicia or your son, bruh. I got both of their ass put up, but I'm not telling you where until you drop my money off to me. I'ma give you the benefit of the doubt to think that you care about her and your junior's life. I need all five of those millions. I got me some investments to make and thangs." He backed up to the doorway of the basement. Meet me at the old train station at midnight with my cash. Don't try no funny shit. If you do, you gon' lose yo people, Phoenix. Mark those words." He looked over to Mikey again. "Midnight, Phoenix." He rushed up the stairs and broke camp out of the back door.

Phoenix rushed to Natalia's side. He helped her to her feet amidst her groaning in agony. As soon as she was upright he wrapped his arms around her body. "Baby, are you okay?" He kissed her lips.

"I'm hurting, daddy. We gotta get me to a hospital fast. I don't feel so good." She held him around the waist. She felt weak and faint.

"Okay, boo, come on then. Daddy got you. You know I do." He wrapped her arm around his neck and guided her from the basement.

***

Mikey waited ten full minutes after all of them had left before he got up. He tore his shirt from him, and peeled off his military issued bullet proof vest made by Kevlar. The vest had been designed specifically for close range attacks, and boy was he thankful for that. He dropped the vest to the ground and ran his hand over the minor wounds on his chest. His back burned from the wounds there as well. His heart began to beat at a rapid pace. "You bitch niggas wanna play games with me. Huh. Awright then, it's on." He grabbed his things off of the floor and fled the basement.

Ghost

***

Natalia stood in front of the last safe that she needed to open before she retrieved the final million dollars to complete the sum total that Smoke needed for the ransom. She didn't feel right. She was thankful that the doctors had told her that her child was safe. She worried that something might have happened to it. Now that she knew she was in the clear, she wanted to get as far away from Memphis, as soon as possible, but she didn't want Alicia to tag along for the ride. She already felt jealous. "Baby, are you sure that we can trust Smoke? What if we give him all of this money and she winds up being dead anyway?"

Phoenix was too busy stuffing the duffle bags with cash. He needed to make five million dollars fit within three bags. "If he plays us, then there is nothing that we can do other than track his ass down and annihilate his ass. But let's just say that he is telling the truth and we can trust him, but we don't pay him the money? Alicia and lil' Phoenix could be dead because of me. That shit will eat at my soul for the rest of my life, and never sit right with me."

Phoenix Jr. Natalia wanted to throw up. She wanted to be the first woman to have Phoenix's junior? She hated Alicia's guts already. She didn't think she could go through with this. Besides, what kind of a female would she be if she paid the ransom just so her man's other baby mother could come back into their lives? A damn idiot of a woman is what she felt. She couldn't do it. She looked at the digital clock hanging on the wall. It read eleven forty. They were ten minutes away from the drop site. She needed to stall.

"Come on, girl, what the fuck is you waiting on?" Phoenix zipped up the second duffle bag and walked over to her.

Natalia squatted down and took a deep breath. "I feel dizzy," she lied. She placed her hand up to the digital keypad, and suddenly fell backward into Phoenix.

Phoenix caught her. He laid her down so he could look her over. Her eyes were closed. She was breathing ruggedly. "Baby, are you okay? What's the matter? Is it the baby?" He placed his hand lightly on her stomach.

Natalia groaned. She opened one eye and glanced at the clock, only five minutes had ticked away from it. She cursed to herself. "My vision Phoenix. I can barely see."

"Damn, what should we do? Should I take you back to the hospital? They did say you should be drinking plenty of fluids. Maybe you need some water." He stood up and rushed into the kitchen to get her some.

Natalia peeked at the clock again. It was eleven forty six. She groaned louder. I think I'm gonna be sick." She jumped up and ran to the bathroom and closed the door, locking it. She lifted the lid of the toilet and faked like she was throwing up. She coughed into the bowl and spit over and over again.

Phoenix appeared with bottled water in his left hand. He tried the door knob and found it locked. He beat on the door. "Lil' Mama, open the door. What the fuck you lock it for?"

Natalia acted like she was still throwing up. She gagged and groaned loudly. "Oh, I feel like shit. I don't want you to see me like this, Phoenix. I need a minute. She gagged loudly.

Phoenix mugged the door. He checked his Patek watch and saw that it was five minutes to midnight. "Fuck. Baby, you gotta give me the combination then. Come on, we got five minutes until midnight. What is it?"

Natalia groaned and gagged into the toilet again. She flushed and ignored him. "Oh, Lord Jesus, help me."

Phoenix beat on the door. "What's the numbers, Natalia? Come on, shawty."

Natalia flushed the toilet again and opened the door looking drained. "I'm in here barely hanging on and all you care about is the money. Wow." She moved him out of the way and slowly walked to the last safe. She knelt down in front of it. "At least I now know what's more important to you." She placed her hand on the five finger print reader, and punched in the eight digit code, before allowing the scanner to read her eyes. It hissed loudly, then the door popped open.

Phoenix took the remaining duffle bag and began to stuff it as fast he could. "You already know I love you more than anybody else. Don't make it seem like this mission is more important than you, because it ain't, but it still has to be accomplished. Now, are you coming with me, or are you staying here?"

Natalia got up with an evil look on her face. "I should be here when you get back."

"Fuck you mean, you should be?" Phoenix was growing irritated as he gazed up at the digital clock on the wall. They were running late, and he was hoping that Smoke wouldn't be on some pure bullshit because of thinking that Natalia and Phoenix had stiffed him.

"I said what I said, Phoenix. You go ahead and handle yo' business. I hope to be here when you get back, but I do have a lot of thinking to do."

Phoenix gazed at the clock again. "Fuck, Natalia. Why are you about to do this shit now?"

Natalia waved him off and headed down the hallway. "Go save that girl, Phoenix. Be careful." She stepped into the main bedroom and slammed the door.

Phoenix mugged the door for a moment. He growled and looked back up at the clock. "Fuck, man."

Chapter 2

It was a hot and humid night, with a full moon in the sky. Smoke checked the clock on his phone, it read twelve oh seven. He adjusted the Draco on his lap, and rubbed his middle finger over the hundred round clip. There was a half mask over his face, and a bullet proof vest across his chest. In the back seat of his nineteen eighty four Chevy Caprice Classic were two of his Orange Mound soldiers that were loyal to him and only him. "Say, mane, if dis mafucka don't show up in ten mo minutes, we finna track his ass down and cut his head off. Y'all hear me?" He looked into his rear view mirror.

Greedy was a dark skinned, nineteen year old savage, with long dreads, and gray eyes. He was born and bred in the Orange Mound, and at nineteen years old, he already had ten bodies under his belt. All he knew was the slums, and he lived for murder and the rebirth. "Say, Smoke, you should've let me wet that fool when I saw his chump ass loafing a few days ago. I had the beam on his temple and every thang. I feel like that was a missed opportunity."

"Shit wasn't ready yet. Mafucka, didn't I tell you that already?" Smoke snapped.

Greedy rubbed his chin. "Yeah, you did, but I'm just saying."

The sound of Phoenix's Escalade wheels was loud on the rocks of the old railway station. Smoke perked up, and squinted his eyes. When he confirmed that it was Phoenix's truck, he sighed in relief. Then he immediately began to look around to make sure that Phoenix didn't have a bunch of bodyguards lurking along with him. "Dats Phoenix right thurr."

"Say the word right now if I'm smoking his bitch ass. You the head of the Cartel, we already know that. Ain't no place for that fool here no mo." Greedy was wired off of the Rebirth and wanted to know what it would feel like to kill a boss like Phoenix. A kill like Phoenix would cement his name in the slums of Memphis as one of the greatest to ever do it. He craved that title.

"Nigga, you don't do shit unless I give you the go ahead. Do you understand me?" Smoke watched Phoenix park his truck so that the headlights were facing his Chevy.

"Yeah, mane, I hear you." Greedy cocked his Mach .90, "but I'm still gon' have this bitch ready just in case." He hit the switch on the military beam, and could taste the salt on his tongue that usually told him that he was getting ready to kill something.

Smoke opened the door to his Chevy and stepped out with both of his killas behind him. He held the Draco in his right hand and watched Phoenix get out of the truck. "Fuck took you so long?"

Phoenix opened the back door to the Escalade. "What other nigga you know gon be able to pull five million dollars out of his ass in a matter of hours? Shit take time, home boy. You know that." He grabbed two of the three duffle bags and dropped them on the ground beside him. "Where is Alicia and Lil' Phoenix?"

Smoke pulled his nose. "How much of my money did you bring? I know how you get down Phoenix."

"Three million, you get your other two when I get Alicia and my son. That's only fair, man. I ain't trying to play you, and all I want is what I'm supposed to get." Phoenix eyed him closely.

"Nigga, that wasn't the deal. The deal was that you bring me five mill, and then I would turn your bitch over to you. Where the fuck is the rest of my money?" Smoke aimed the Draco at him.

18

A red beam appeared from the east side of the railway yard. The red dot landed on Smoke's forehead, and then there was a dot for both of his guys that stood behind him. Phoenix stepped up to Smoke. "Look, bruh, I know you got kill feelings toward me, but fuck yo feelings, nigga. Where is my bitch, and my seed? You don't tell me what's good, we both are about to die tonight."

Smoke felt like a damn fool. "This how you getting down?"

"I knew you should've let me Smoke his bitch ass. That nigga got snake running all through his DNA." Greedy wanted to risk it all by airing at Phoenix. He was high as a cloud.

"Nigga, you can have this three million? Just tell me where my bitch is?" Phoenix watched as two more beams appeared on Smoke's forehead.

Smoke was so heated that he began to shake. "You got me, nigga. I slipped. He reached down and grabbed the bags off of the ground. He held them in one hand. "Yo bitch and yo son in the trunk. Both got oxygen masks on. Grab they ass before shit gets out of hand here." Smoke made his way to the driver's side of his car. He popped the trunk.

Phoenix took off running to the back of it. Sure enough, both Alicia and Junior were in the back of the trunk with oxygen masks on their faces. When Alicia saw Phoenix she began to scream her head off into the mask that was taped to her face. Junior was still. "Shit, get out of here. Come on." He pulled Alicia out of the trunk. She fell to the ground, her legs were jelly.

"Hurry up and get them, Phoenix, I gotta be out," Smoke hollered.

Phoenix grabbed Junior out of the car, just before Smoke stepped on the gas and stormed out of the railway yard. Phoenix fell to his knees with his son in his arms. He took the mask and duct tape off of his mouth and kissed all over the baby. "Phoenix, Phoenix, wake up, baby. Wake up," he hollered.

Alicia came over to him and placed her face in front of him. She screamed into the mask and duct tape again. Phoenix pulled both off and cast them to the ground. Alicia took a deep breath of air. She fell back to her knees. "They killed him, Phoenix. He's dead. That baby been dead," she wailed.

"What?" Phoenix stood up with his son. "Phoenix, Phoenix, wake up, baby. Wake up. He held up his phone and shined the light of it on to Junior's face. It was blue just like his lips. Tears dropped from Phoenix's eyes. "How long, Alicia? How long has my son been dead?" he asked with his voice breaking up.

"Five hours, at least. Smoke did it. He choked our son out, talking about killing your seed before he could turn into you. I was trying to tell you that before you let his ass go." She took Phoenix Jr. from his arms.

Phoenix watched Smoke's brake lights disappear down the street. The car stopped at the traffic lights before Smoke turned right and disappeared from his view. Phoenix felt tears roll down his eyes. He nodded his head in anger. Smoke had to die, and not just Smoke. Because of what Smoke had done, he'd opened the gates of hell. That meant that everybody that Phoenix even thought Smoke cared about had to go, kids and all. Phoenix looked down at Alicia as she held his son. She cried her eyes out, asking why. He felt his heart turning colder and colder the more he listened to her weep.

***

"Three muthafuckin' million dollars, nigga. Three million, plus the five hundred thousand we got from Mikey, so that's what?" Greedy couldn't count that high.

"Three point five million, ignorant ass nigga. Damn, yo ass need an education or something," Tyson laughed. He was five feet nine inches tall, brown skinned, with brown eyes and prominent muscles all over his body. He was Smoke crazy, his loyalty for Smoke was unmatched.

"Fuck you, nigga. Who needs an education when we have all that money over there? Smoke made it happen once again." Greedy grabbed a ten thousand stack of the bread, and thumbed through it. He was already spending it in his mind.

Smoke walked into the basement with twin Glocks in his belt. He snatched the money out of Greedy's hands. "Go sit yo ass over there for a minute, Joe. Let me fuck wit you nigga's mentals for a minute."

Greedy was stuck. "Fuck wit' my what?"

Tyson lowered his head and shook it. "Damn, that shit doesn't make no sense. Bruh, he said he wanna put something on our minds."

"Aw, well hell, why didn't you just say that?" Greedy asked. He took a seat on the couch and sparked a blunt that was stuffed with Purple Haze.

Smoke dropped the ten thousand dollars into the duffle bag again. "I want us to level up. I'm tired of niggas from the Mound hurting the way that we are, and I'm tired of them Black Haven niggas being on our heels. I'm ready to take shit to the next level in a major way. I'm ready for all of us to get paid in a way that we ain't never been paid before. To be able to do that, it means that we have to invest all of this money into the hood and our people. In a year's time, we should be able to see the residuals."

"A year? Fuck you talking bout, potna? Mafuckas got bills right now, and I don't give a fuck about what happens a year from now, or nobody else in the Mound, if they ain't in this room. I'm trying to get mine right now. Fuck the dumb shit," Greedy snapped, standing up.

"That's how you feel, too, Tyson?" Smoke wanted to know what kind of men he was dealing with.

"I mean, I am tired of being broke, and my family does have bills like right now, but at the same time, I'm all about that long term money, too. I got a few of my potnas that do that studio shit real tough but can't get any financial backing. If I had a lil' cash, I can open studios, and use a few of my plugs out in New York and put their ass on. On the flip side of that, I got dope boys running all through my fam as well. So really I just need to know what you are driving at?"

"I'll tell you what, me and you are going to sit down and come up with a plan on how we're going to go about putting them on. Once we get that shit settled, then I'll fuck with this other shit I got going on in my head. Far as you go, Greedy." Smoke grabbed the duffle bag and took ten minutes to place five hundred thousand dollars in Greedy's lap. "This is yours right here. Spend it how you want to, and when all of it is gone, come and tell me what you did with it. I'm letting you know now that I forgive you ahead of time."

Greedy nodded his head. "Yep, it sounds good to me. I earned it." He got up and began to compile the money in front of him. "You got a pillowcase or something?"

Smoke grabbed a laundry bag off of the dryer. He handed it to Greedy. "Here, lil' dawg. Both of y'all listen up, instead of us taking over the Duffle Bag Cartel, we gon start our own shit with me at the head. We are officially about our bread from this point on, right?"

Tyson nodded. "Hell yeah, we are. We ain't got no other choice other than to be about that cash."

Greedy stuffed stack after stack of money into his bag. "You already know that don't shit else matters to me."

"Well dis is Memphis, and we from the Mound. You two are the first of many members of the Bread Gang Cartel." Smoke eyed them with laser focus. "We are about to get money in a major way. And all I ask is that the both of you follow my commands, ready to die." He tossed Tyson ten thousand dollars. "This ought to hold you off until you present your vision before me. Bread Gang, nigga."

Tyson smiled. "Bread Gang."

Greedy draped his sack of money over his shoulders. "Bread Gang, niggas. Now let's take over the slums."

***

Mikey made it into his house and fell on the floor as soon as he stepped on the welcome mat. Ivy ran to his side and dropped down in front of him. "Oh my God, Mikey, what's the matter? What happened to you?" She was hysterical.

Mikey looked up at her and scrunched his face. "Call up my cousin Slugger for me and tell him to bring every last one of his killas from New Orleans and get their monkey ass over here to Memphis. Mafuckas trying to take over the Cartel. Well, I ain't going. Call him now, Ivy," he hollered, and closed his eyes in excruciating pain. Revenge plagued his mind. Phoenix's face was a consistent figure floating through his mental, and then Smoke's. Betrayal was fresh on his soul. He felt like screaming from the torture of it. He took a deep breath, and slowly blew it out. "You reap what you sow, niggas. I swear to God you will."

Chapter 3
Six months later...

Smoke dropped the top on his black and white Porsche and cruised down the strip of Orange Mound. There was a black van with four shooters that followed behind his Porsche, ready to protect Smoke, and anybody riding with him, at all costs.

Smoke ran his tongue over his gold grill. He'd placed a quarter carat diamond in each tooth. Every time the sun reflected off of the jewels, they shined brightly. He scanned the strip through his Chanel gold frames and adjusted the Mach .90 on his lap. It was a brisk March day in twenty-twenty. All along the strip were dope boys standing out, getting large sums of cash from the dope addicts that were addicted to the heroin that Smoke personally put together himself, after securing a steady plug out of Sinaloa, Mexico. The dope didn't jump as hard as the Rebirth, but it was the next best thing, and he was getting money to the fullest. He slowed the Porsche and lowered his sunglasses.

"Say, mane, it's about eight too many in this hurr group right hurr. Y'all need to break that shit up before twelve spin through dis Bitch and give me a hard time. We are supposed to be working smarter, not harder, you feel me?"

The group slowly parted with their sacks on them. Greedy mugged them with anger beaming inside of him. "Say, mane, I done told these niggas how you only want the trappers working in two's. Dese niggas hard headed, dat and mafuckas worried about when Mikey gone strike. They say he was rolling through this bitch ten trucks deep with them heavy hitters out of New Orleans."

Smoke pulled away from the curb. "I still can't believe that Phoenix didn't kill that sucka ass nigga. Somethin' told me to handle my bidness myself. Now I gotta worry about

Phoenix and Mikey. That shit get in the way of my decision making at times." He rolled past six of Orange Mound's finest honeys. They waved at him and switched their asses that were encased in the tightest pairs of Capri pants that they could find. Their asses jiggled like Jello. All of them were thick and known for fuckin' dope boys to sleep. Smoke felt a tingle in his dick. He slowed the whip. Shawty, y'all Facebook me in a minute and I'm finna see what you hoes on. Awright?"

They were giddy, and nodded at him in unison.

A strapped redbone with short, curly hair stepped forward with red lipstick, and green contacts in her eyes. She licked her lips, and rested her arm on the window seal of his Porsche. "Say, Smoke, when you gon' scoop a bitch up and see what's really good wit' me? You got all of these other hoes checking a bag in one way or the other, when I got all of this mafuckin' talent. I can pop that that thang you got thurr on yo' lap, or I can pop this thang right here on a mafucka lap for that cash, too." She turned around and made her ass cheeks jiggle inside of her Capri pants. The globes were juicy.

Smoke licked his lips and cheesed. "Shawty, how old you is?"

"Seventeen, but ain't a mafucka caring out hurr. Dis Memphis, age ain't nothin' but a number. Besides, I'll be eighteen in a few weeks. I'm tryna have my money right before den."

"What dat name is again?" Smoke looked over her body and imagined fucking her from the back while she called him daddy. He loved lil' young strapped hoes. He just couldn't help himself.

"Precious Love." She batted her eyes at him. "That's exactly what I can be to you, too, daddy."

Smoke's dick jumped. "Say, mane, hit my Facebook, and I'ma fuck wit you. Show me how persistent you are, and I'ma put yo' lil' ass on. That's my word. What are you good at?"

"I can do hair. I can dance. I can shake my ass. I can get on that thang between dem legs and ride that bitch, too. I'm trained and ready to go. I'm seventeen but dese my girls that run under me. We 'bout that paper, but we are trying to be down with the Bread Gang, just like everybody else in Memphis who wants better for themselves."

Smoke smiled. "Greedy, I like lil' mama." He laughed and turned back to Precious. "Shake that ass for me one more time."

Precious turned around and spaced her thick thighs. She waved her ass from side to side, then bent all the way over and twerked for Smoke. Her globes were jiggling so hard that her pants came down to reveal the red thong that separated her ass cheeks. Light hair could be seen on her yellow skin.

Smoke was hard as a rock. He had to fuck her, but he was gone play it cool. "Like I said, shawty, you hit me up on Facebook, and I'ma fuck wit' you. You got my word on that." He pulled away from the curb again.

Greedy turned his head back so he could see her one more time. "Mane, I'd risk catching a case to fuck her lil' thick ass. I know she got some good pussy. Some hoes you just know they do, and that lil' bitch most definitely do."

Smoke laughed. "Dawg what's wit' these lil' bitches? They are just getting more and more strapped, it seems like. They be young as hell, too." Smoke shook his head.

"And I am taking their ass down. Straight up. Ain't nothin' like fresh pussy. Show me any nigga that don't think about smashing a lil' young bitch, and I'll show you a nigga who I'd punch straight in his shit for lying." Greedy was serious.

Smoke was dying laughing, though he was still on point of his surroundings. "Every nigga wit that young pussy, mane, they just keep that shit to themselves. Just like every nigga love that vet pussy. Older hoes be on bidness, too, now."

Smoke had a thing for vet pussy. Once a female hit thirty and up, he automatically assumed they were ferocious in the sack.

"I'm good on that. I like my car wit' no miles on it. No hair, and no miles. Hell yeah, matter fact, I'm finna set it up so I can fuck a bunch of young hoes tonight. They got some prom shit going on anyway, and I'm finna poach they lil' asses." Greedy got to texting away on his phone with a big smile on his face.

"Yeah, well as soon as Precious hit me up, I'ma buss her lil' ass down and put her up for a few weeks until she flipped eighteen. I'll be damn if they catch me slipping like that. Tennessee be jamming niggas up for that young pussy."

"That's why I gotta have it. I'm finna throw an Orange Mound prom after-party. Bitches gotta show me their high school ID in order to get in." He was serious, and already setting it up.

Smoke kept rolling. "You wilding, but that's you though. Tyson and the music industry side of the Bread Gang leave for a eight city tour tomorrow night. Before they do, I gotta get my ducks in a row with him." His phone vibrated. He looked at the face and saw that Precious was sending him a friend request. He accepted it and knew he would be fucking her before the night was out.

"Why you stop talking, nigga?" Greedy mugged him.

"Aw, then we gon hit up the traps and collect my money, after that, you can go to your party, and I'ma fuck wit shawty lil' thick ass. I'll get at you later on. Bet those?"

"Bet those, nigga."

***

Mikey took a hammer and slammed it into the center of a kilogram of imported China White. The dope cracked but didn't break apart. Mikey slammed it again with the hammer, and finally it broke into twelve big chunks. He scooted his chair closer to the table and breathed through his mask as best he could. His nose was stopped up because he had a cold. Memphis was experiencing the worst flu season in years, and with the Coronavirus running rampant all over the United States, Mikey was just a tad bit nervous.

He slid the platter of heroin down the table where six of his workers began to dismantle it by breaking it apart, weighing it up, and aluminum foiling the product to Mikey's liking. Though Mikey had a few hundred thousand put up, he had a weakness for the trap. He loved to be inside of it, grinding with his underlings. But today, his cold was kicking his ass. "Say, mane, this the tenth kee right here we're breaking down. After we get this shit weighed and bagged, y'all go make the drop offs, and we'll be right back here at eight o'clock tomorrow, on the same shit. Any questions?"

There were none.

"Good." He stood up and removed his gloves. He had a pounding headache, and his stomach was feeling upset. He staggered into the bathroom and closed the door. "Damn, I hope I ain't getting sick." He knelt to one knee and made himself throw up. After finishing, he took a sip from a portable bottle of mouthwash, and swished it around inside of his mouth, before spitting it back in the toilet. He looked at his eyes in the mirror. They were bloodshot. He felt weak. "Damn." He felt sweat pour from his forehead.

Ivy knocked on the door, and placed her ear to it. She was light skinned with natural curly hair, and hazel eyes. She was thick as a choke sandwich. "Mikey, you okay in there?"

"Nall, shawty, I'm sick as hell. I think I need to lay my ass down or something."

"You need to go to the hospital, Mikey. You have the flu. Every time I run this damn thermometer over your head, it's boiling. How many more signs do you need?"

Mikey felt dizzy. "Shawty, I ain't tryna have yo ass nagging me right now."

Ivy twisted the knob and stepped into the bathroom. She closed the door behind her. Mikey stood holding himself by the wall. His clothes were drenched in sweat. His face was a reddish brown. He was struggling to remain upright and Ivy could tell.

"Holy shit, Mikey, we gotta get you to a hospital right now before you pass out." She rubbed his back. "Let me see your face."

Mikey moved her away from him. "I ain't going to nobody's hospital. I ain't sick, I'm just a little jet lagged." His mouth was dry.

"Mikey, you've been back from Hong Kong for two weeks. You shouldn't still be jet lagged. There is something else going on."

Mikey closed his eyes. His head was spinning. He began to perspire worse than he ever had. "You gotta drive me to my crib so I can take a cold bath. We gotta leave out the back, too? I don't want mafuckas seeing me all weak and shit, not with all of this shit going on. You got me?"

"Baby, you should be going to the hospital, not home. Let me take you there."

Mikey grabbed her by the throat. "What I say, bitch? Huh? Didn't I say take me home? Huh? You need to do what the fuck I say, and not tell me what you think I should do, because that a get you fucked up. Are you feeling me right now?" He was dizzy and lethargic.

Ivy mugged him. She could barely breathe. She nodded her head. "Let me go."

Mikey released her and fell backward. He thought he was about to stop and catch his balance but he kept falling backward until he tripped over the lip of the tub and hit his head on the porcelain. Blood ran down his neck. "Aw fuck, shawty." His eyes rolled into the back of his head for a moment.

Ivy began to panic. "What do I do? What do I do? Shit, Mikey, what do I do?" She felt like she was on the verge of freaking out. Blood drenched his shirt from the wound. Ivy reached into the tub and pulled him forward so she could look into his scalp. There was a two inch gash that was spitting up blood. His body felt as hot as lava. "Mikey, baby, can you hear me?"

Mikey was so dizzy that he could barely see. He closed his eyes. His mouth was drier than sand paper. He opened his eyes back and saw two of Ivy. "Baby, I need some drank. I need some Codeine. That syrup'll get a mafucka right." He smiled, and closed his eyes. He tried to get up but fell back down.

Ivy held her hands to her face. "Baby, I think I gotta go and get you some help. You don't look good at all, and you're bleeding profusely."

"Shawty, don't you take yo ass out there and tell them niggas from Naw'lins that a mafucka weak. They a pounce on a nigga. I got this shit. Just help me up." He held his hands out for her.

Ivy wrapped her arms around his sweaty body and pulled him up. "Come on."

He coughed and threw up on her chest, then messed his pants. "I'm fucked up, Ivy." He fainted.

Ivy bent beside him and fanned his face. "Mikey. Baby. Wake up. Wake up, baby. Please." She looked around. She didn't know what to do or think. She felt the side of his face. It was burning up.

Mikey already had a hundred and three fever, and it was set to climb higher. His nose began to bleed. The Coronavirus had slowly broken down his immune system and was now running rampant inside of him, attacking him internally. Mikey began to shake.

"Mikey, I know you're going to be mad at me but I don't care. I gotta get you to the hospital so we can see what is wrong wit' you boy. I would never forgive myself if you died on my accord." Ivy ran out of the bathroom and grabbed two of Mikey's hittas.

It took them five minutes to get him into the truck with him fighting them the whole way. It took twenty minutes to get him to the hospital. Before he got there, he threw up two more times, and messed himself again. It took the doctors one hour to diagnose the Coronavirus in his system, and another eight minutes before they ordered him to be quarantined. At the hearing of his fate, Mikey passed out and whispered that he was going to kill Ivy when they finally released him.

Chapter 4

"Phoenix, get off of me. She went right down the hall. She will hear us if we get started. Besides, my man is sitting in the living room." Sabrina tried to knock Phoenix's hands from pulling up her skirt.

Phoenix wasn't trying to hear what she was talking about. He pressed her body against the wall, and slid his hands under her skirt again. He cupped her fat ass cheeks and groaned into her neck. Her skin was hot. Her perfume mixed with her natural scent was driving him crazy.

"Man fuck dude, Sabrina, we family. I come before any nigga you meet." He slid his hands into her panties from front and felt her bald, moist lips. He peeled them open and tried to slide his middle finger into her.

Sabrina moaned, and pushed at him again. "Phoenix, boy gone. He's a good man. Do you know how hard it is to find a good man nowadays?"

Phoenix sucked her neck. "Nope, shawty, I ain't been looking for one." He dropped down and yanked her skirt up. Her panties were pulled to the side of her sex lips exposing them. They were golden, and full of dew. From his knees, Phoenix could smell the headiness of her arousal. He kissed her pussy and slid his tongue up and down her slit while holding the sex lips wide open. Her clitoris sat at the top of her split like an erect nipple begging for attention. He sucked it, and flicked it three times fast with his tongue.

Sabrina groaned deep within her throat. She squeezed her eyes tight, and inadvertently humped into his mouth to feel him better. She thought about Kevin in the other room, and how their relationship was progressing for the better. He was such a gentleman, so conscious of her emotional needs. She arched her back as she felt Phoenix peel her booty cheeks open and swipe his tongue up and down in between them. He sucked on her rosebud. She dug her nails into his shoulders.

"Cuz, you thick as a muthafucka. That nigga don't know how to handle this thick ass. You need a mafucka to beat this pussy up. This my bloodline, I know what's good." He slipped two fingers into her tight gap and ran them in and out slowly. He sucked them into his mouth, and savored the flavor of her.

Sabrina watched Phoenix and began to tremble. She couldn't believe that he was so nasty, and brazen. It caused her pussy to drool. "Phoenix, please stop. We said we weren't gon' do this shit no more. We're supposed to be family."

Phoenix picked her up into the air and set her down on the dresser. Now she was at the perfect height for him to do what he needed to do. She held his shoulders while he stood between her legs and kissed all over her pussy. "He played with the lips. "Look at how fat this mafucka is. You telling me that a nigga outside of this blood I got flowing through me can fuck this pussy the right way? Huh?"

He slurped her juices that were oozing out of her. He squeezed the lips together, and sipped from her crease. Then he opened her wide, and manipulated her clitoris for five straight minutes doing everything that he could think of that would drive her crazy.

Sabrina shivered. She bucked. She bit into her arm to keep from screaming out loud. Her eyes rolled backward, and then she was cumming so hard that she felt faint afterward. Her juices ran down Phoenix's neck. She kicked him away and got up on wobbly legs. "Phoenix, okay, cuz. Now we gotta stop. It doesn't look right. We've been in here too long." She wiped sweat from her forehead.

Phoenix opened his Chanel jeans, and showed her his piece. It throbbed hungrily. The big head was a purplish color full of excitement.

"You finna gimme some of that pussy." He closed the distance in between them, and pulled her to him. His piece stuck right into her middle.

Sabrina tried to fight him off. "Get off of me." She didn't want to risk losing Kevin.

Phoenix picked her up and tossed her on the bed. She yelped. He climbed between her thick thighs, and yanked her panties from her with one strong tug. He threw them against the wall. She pushed at him. He grabbed a hold of his dick and ran the head up and down her slippery slit, before he sunk into her heat. She was tight. She sucked at him. He pushed forward and buried his dick as deep as it could go. Once his balls were sitting on the crack of her ass, he moaned.

Sabrina popped her legs wide open. She could feel Phoenix deep within her belly. She couldn't believe that he was fucking her again. "Damn you, Phoenix."

Phoenix pulled her closer by use of her hips, and began to fuck her hard, with no mercy. "Uh. Uh. This my pussy. Fuck yo nigga. Fuck yo nigga. Uh. Uh."

"Mmm. Mmm. Mmm. Stop, shit." Sabrina closed her eyes. Her tongue traced her lips. She sucked her bottom one, and moaned louder, recklessly. It felt so good, and so wrong at the same time.

Phoenix watched his dick go in and out of her. He thought back to when they were just kids and they would be under the bed screwing while their parents were in the living room playing Spades. Phoenix would be sucking all over Sabrina's breasts that were just coming in, while his small penis slammed into her bald coochie. Even back then, she would get so wet that she would have his drawers soaked. He would always be worried that their parents would know what they had done. Sabrina would beg him to rub between her little legs while she pumped his piece, fascinated by the thing that he had and she didn't.

Phoenix groaned as he felt her cat grip him just as her small fist used to. He pumped harder, and bit into her neck to purposely leave a mark.

Sabrina humped upward into him and gasped as she felt him enter into her lower belly. She cocked her thighs wide open and came, digging her nails into his shoulder blades. "Uhhhh. Un-uh. Shit." She fell back on the bed.

Phoenix kept stroking. He could feel his nut building. He was close. He could feel it. He placed her left thick thigh on his shoulder and sucked on it while he plunged into that forbidden pussy. Sabrina rubbed his abs. She sat up and sucked his lip, and fell back.

"They're there playing cards, Phoenix," she whispered. "Our parents are playing cards." She knew Phoenix's triggers. She wanted to take him back to their childhood. He never ceased to cum faster whenever she did that.

Phoenix trembled, and fucked her faster. He long stroked her now. She got tighter. She grabbed a pillow from the bed and screamed into it. Phoenix opened his eyes to watch his dick attacking her cat. Her golden lips were a reddish color now, they were fully engorged. "I'm close, Sabrina. I'm close, cuz." He cocked back as far as he could. The tip of his dick head came to the edge of her sex lips before he slammed it back home and began to long stroke her.

" Arrgh." Sabrina bit into the pillow again and came.

"Shit. Shit. Shit." Phoenix felt his pleasures mounting. He was seconds away from cumming. The scent of Sabrina's pussy was loud in the room. It was enough to drive him sexually mad.

Kevin stepped to the bedroom door and knocked four times. "Baby, are you okay in there?"

Sabrina pushed Phoenix off of her, and slipped from the bed with her cum and juices running down her golden thighs. She pulled her short skirt down as far as it could go. Her ass poked out of it like a beer belly. "Yeah, honey, I'm just hollering at my cousin. I told you how crazy he is. I'll be out there in a minute."

Phoenix was out of the bed. He forced her up against the wall and yanked her skirt back up. He slid into her from the back and began fucking at full speed. His dick burrowed through her crease again and again, stretching her wide.

"Yeah, because I need to get back to the studio. I got a few artists that just arrived from Memphis and I need to give them my undivided attention. Baby, I can tell that they are going to be stars. Before I go, I need to kiss those sexy lips. You know you're my good luck charm."

Phoenix pounded her out as fast and as hard as he could. He closed his eyes and came squeezing her booty, and pulling her back into him while he fucked her. Sabrina still had that bomb and there was no way that he was about to pass it up just because she was fucking with somebody. Phoenix pulled out and came in between her ass cheeks and all over her globes. He stood back stroking his piece.

Sabrina hurried to the door. "Okay, baby, I'll be out in one second. Here I come." She glared at Phoenix.

He shrugged his shoulders. "What?"

***

It was a bright and sunny day in the city of Miami. Natalia sat back in the passenger's seat of Phoenix's cherry red Hellcat, allowing her long, curly hair to blow in the wind. Her Dolce and Gabbana shades were gold framed and made her look like a flawless movie star.

She sipped diet Pepsi from her straw and sighed in irritation. "Phoenix, it's been six months. What are we doing?" She rested her hand on her big belly. She was due to have their son in a month. While she was excited to finally have the child outside of her body, she worried about how the delivery would go.

"Shawty, what yo' lil' ass over thurr talking 'bout now?"

"You know it's not what I'm talking about, but who I'm talking about? When are we going to buy Alicia her own place so she can get the fuck off of my throne? I don't like sharing my house with some other female. It defeats the purpose. And besides all of that, you're the only one that's having your cake and eating it, too." She rolled her eyes.

"Here you go wit' this bullshit, Natalia. You know that girl ain't ready to be out and about on her own. We just lost a child. You think she bounced back from that already?"

Natalia shrugged her shoulders. "I don't know, and to be honest with you, that is not my problem to dwell on. You and I need to be getting ready to have this baby. Our baby. She gotta get the fuck out of my house. That's all there is to it. Now, I'll put her up in her own shit. It's all kinds of houses that she can pick from, but she gotta go. It's as simple as that."

Phoenix kept rolling. "Damn, you cold as ice, Natalia. The girl just lost a baby. She needs time to grieve."

Natalia scrunched her face. "You did, too. Why don't you need so much time to grieve then? I mean, after all, just like it was her child, supposedly, it was yours as well. So tell me why you ain't down in the dumps like she is?"

"Man, you already know that my heart is as cold as ice. Even though I loved my child with her, I didn't get a chance to form a relationship with him, so there were very few feelings attached to him. But she was his mother. She carried him in her womb for nine months, and then gave birth. Her connection was stronger, and deeper than mine could've ever been."

Natalia nodded her head. "Damn, I didn't even think about it like that." She was quiet for a moment. "Still in all though, I don't like no bitch around my nigga all the time. I hate staying up as long as I can because I think you're about to slip off down the hall so you can fuck her as soon as I got to sleep. That shit gets irritating."

"That's cuz you're stressing yourself out over nothing. It ain't even like that."

"Like what?" Natalia pulled a strand of hair out of her face and looked over to him.

"Whatever you think we are doing, we ain't been on none of that shit. I've been trying to get her head right so that when it's time for her to go off on her own, she'll be good. Other than that, we just were cool. That's all."

Natalia looked at him like he was stupid. "Phoenix, you must think that I am still that lil' stupid ass red bone you knocked up in Russia or somethin'. What, you don't think I got enough common sense to know what you were on with Alicia? Really?"

"I don't know what you're talking about."

"How many times, Phoenix?"

"How many times what?" Phoenix looked over at her with an angry look on his face.

"How many times have you fucked her since we been in Miami? Keep that shit one hunnit?"

"Man, get your mind out of the gutter. I ain't been on that. I have told you what it is with me and her. Now calm yo lil' ass down." He pulled off of the freeway and headed toward the mansions off of South Beach.

"So you gon sit yo burnt caramel ass there and really say y'all ain't on shit, right? That's what you're telling me?"

He smiled and gave her both dimples. "What more do you want me to say? It is what it is."

She nodded her head. "Okay, Phoenix, we're going to leave this conversation right here. But if I find out that anything is cracking between you and her, we're going to have a serious problem. That bitch is, too, because you are my blood. And just like your heart is cold, my heart is as cold as ice, especially when a mafucka takes my kindness for weakness. Now get me home so I can lay down. You're giving me a mafuckin' migraine."

Phoenix looked over at her and laughed. "Yo lil' ass done got ratchet as hell since you were out of Russia. That black side all out of yo monkey ass now." He snickered. "Baby all nigga now." He cracked.

"Yeah, and you gon' see a whole lot more if I find out you're lying to me about this bitch. That's on everything. Now I'm giving you this last chance to tell me what the fuck y'all got going on? Are you sleeping with her?"

Phoenix smiled. "Natalia, if you don't calm yo lil' yellow ass down so that my baby that's growing inside of you can have some peace, we're about to have a serious misunderstanding." It was the best he could do to avoid her question. He hoped it worked.

Natalia nodded her head and sucked her teeth. "Okay, Phoenix, we'll have it your way. I'm cool. It's all good." She rested her arm on the seal of the window and sat back.

Every time she imagined Alicia's face, she felt a surge of anger come over her. Alicia had to go. That's all there was to it. It was the only way she could ever see herself getting any peace, and that went for the child that she was carrying inside of her as well.

"Shawty, I think every thang gonna work out for the best. We gon get you home, and I'ma rub them lil' pretty feet and we're going to go from there. Awright."

"Yeah, nigga, awright."

"Wit yo ratchet ass." He busted up laughing.

Ghost

Chapter 5

Alicia stood in the full length mirror in just a pair of white lace boy shorts, and the matching bra that was see through. She eyed her frame from head to toe, before rubbing her belly. She thought about Phoenix Junior and became weary. She sighed in depression. Though it had been six months, it still felt to her as if it were yesterday. She imagined his little smile. The deep dimples that were on each of his cheeks, and her depression seemed to grow stronger. Suddenly she felt weak. Why did bad things have to happen to good people? She wondered.

Phoenix knocked on the door once before slipping inside of the bedroom. He stepped behind her and wrapped her into his arms. "Hey, lil' lady, how are you feeling?"

Alicia closed her eyes and smiled. "Better now. How are you doing?"

"I got a lot of shit on my plate for the next few days, but I just wanted to take some time out to check on you. You look like you're getting thicker, though. You've been eating?"

She rolled her eyes. "That's all you ever see is what a female's body looks like. What about the things that are going on inside of my mind and my heart, Phoenix? Do any of those matter?" She broke away from him and walked toward the bed with her supple cheeks jiggling like crazy. The boy shorts were all up in her crack, and to Phoenix, that looked so good.

"Damn, why are you coming down on me so hard? I thought I was at the very least your friend." He followed her to the bed and stood in front of her. Her thighs were freshly oiled and shining. One glance to her feet showcased the nails there that were recently done. Alicia, as always, was well put together.

"So now we're just friends," she scoffed. "Typical. I guess I'm only more than that when you want something from me."

Phoenix sat beside her. "Alicia, guess what, Goddess?"

She side eyed him. "What, Phoenix?"

"I love you, and you are more than a friend to me. You're my baby." He tried to kiss her on the cheek.

Alicia moved out of his reach. "I have already heard you call Natalia your baby on countless occasions. It's to the point that I don't even wanna hear those words come out of your mouth. They sicken me. Speaking of Natalia, she sent you in here, huh? She wanna know when I'll be ready to move out of y'all lil' set up here, don't she?" Alicia stood up.

Phoenix lowered his head. The bright sunlight shined in through Alicia's window. He stood up. "Y'all ain't been jamming ever since our shorty passed away. I know you don't like her, and I don't wanna say the feeling is mutual, but I mean, how can it not be?"

"You know what Phoenix, I'm done with being weak. I wanna find my own shit, and I wanna be out of y'all lil' mansion by the end of this week. You got all of this fuckin' pull and connections, then why don't you plug me with a nice place like this somewhere?"

"Like this? Girl, you tripping. Fuck I look like buying you a mansion? What type of gwop do you think I'm working with?"

She mugged him. "Aw, I get it. Natalia gets to have a mansion because she is about to have your baby, and she is also a little lighter than me. Everybody knows how Phoenix likes his lil' red hoes. But yeah, since this girl is about to give birth to your son, and the son we had together is now deceased, that means that she can live in a mansion, and I get what, an apartment. The sun has darkened my skin some, and I do not currently possess a baby by yo trifling ass. So what do I get, a studio apartment?" She stepped into his face.

Phoenix made out the hard nipples that were sticking through her bra. He looked her over. "You can have whatever you want. That's why I'm still in the game and checking a big bag on a daily basis. Don't come at me wit' that light skinned shit, though. You ain't so mafuckin' dark yourself, to be playing that card."

"Yeah, whatever. So you gon' buy me a mansion like this, huh? Am I gonna have four bedrooms with three and a half baths?"

"Fuck you gon' need all other space for? It's just you."

She stepped closer. "I might wanna host a party to get to know some people. Or I might wanna invite my whole family over. Now that they know I ain't screwing with Mikey no more, everybody has been trying to hit me up to see what's good with me. I ain't responded, but sooner or later, I might, seeming as yo' black ass got a whole family you're about to head. Who do I have left, Phoenix? Who?"

"What?" Phoenix was confused.

"You're damn right. All I got is me. And if I wanna live in a big old mansion all by my lonely, then I will, because don't a muthafucka really care about Alicia. All Alicia got is herself. And I'm sick of it." Her eyes became watery. She turned her back to him before a tear dropped. She couldn't allow him to see her in such a vulnerable state.

Phoenix felt hurt. He took a hold of her and turned her around so that she was facing him. "Alicia, what's the matter, baby?"

"Don't call me baby, Phoenix. Please don't. I don't ever want to hear you call me that ever again. My name is not baby, it's Alicia."

"Man, fuck that. I call you what I wanna call you, and I'm calling you baby. Now tell me what's wrong with you?"

"You're what's wrong with me, Phoenix. Your country ass. You bring me all the way here from Memphis, for what? So I can live in your guest bedroom? What is your endgame here, because I'm not seeing one that makes sense for anybody other than you?"

"I don't have an end game, Alicia. I thought we all were going to live in harmony. I didn't know y'all was going to hate each other."

"Oh so now that girl hates me?" Alicia was offended. "For what? What did I do to her for her to feel a way about me? I have been nothing but kind and respectful to her, and you. What more can I do?"

Natalia pushed open the door and stepped into the room. Phoenix backed away from Alicia. Natalia mugged him. Then she turned her gaze to Alicia. "You got somethin' you wanna say to me?" She took two more steps into the room, her pregnant belly leading the way.

Alicia came around and stood a few feet from her. "Why do you hate me? What did I do to you for you to feel so ill toward me?"

"Who said that I hated you? I don't even know you well enough to feel that strongly toward you." Natalia eyed Phoenix.

Alicia mugged him as well. "Look, I know that you and Phoenix are together. I get that, and I respect that. Since I was here, I haven't tried to step on your toes, or to break you two apart. I've stayed in my own lane and allowed myself to grieve over my child. But now that it's clear that you want me out, I would like to have his help in finding me a place where I can live just as comfortably as this. I mean, after all, I did have his child as well. Why shouldn't I be able to?"

Natalia laughed. "This mansion cost every bit of six million dollars, and that was after a bit of haggling to get the real estate agent to drop one point five off of the price tag."

Alicia stepped closer. "And? What are you saying? You think that I don't deserve something as luxurious? Really?" Alicia grew angry.

Natalia laughed again. "You're funny."

"Bitch, why am I funny?" Alicia snapped, ready to hop on to Natalia's ass.

"Because you thought that Phoenix dropped the money for us to live in this mansion. Girl, yeah right." She cracked up.

Phoenix glared at her. "Shut yo ass up. That shit ain't that funny."

"First off, I don't need no man taking care of me, or doing shit for me that I can do for myself. That's why I laughed. Another reason is because even though I love Phoenix and I'll die with him any day of the week, his bread ain't up like that to be buying no mansions and stuff. So if you wanna live like this, you gon' have to either get it on your own, or I'll get it for you and you can just pay me back. What are you good at?"

Alicia was taken aback. Natalia was throwing a lot at her at one time. "What do you mean what am I good at?"

"What can you do?" Natalia looked up at Phoenix. He was heated, and she could see that. She didn't care.

"I do hair. I can cook really well. I am very business minded. I have a degree in culinary arts, and cosmetology. I can do nails. I mean what are you looking for here?"

"We gon' test that theory. As a favor to you, I'ma open you up to all three." Natalia rubbed her stomach.

"All three what?" Alicia looked her over, and then up to Phoenix.

"Girl, what I'm saying is that I am willing to help you get on your feet by opening you up three businesses that you can run. I mean, in a perfect world, we would start off with just one. But I see how you were able to sit up for six months and stew deep within your thoughts. I can only imagine that you were putting together a game plan."

"I might've been." Alicia lowered her eyes. "Wait a minute, so you're telling me that you're willing to invest in me, even though you hate me? That makes no sense."

"You need to stop listening to Phoenix because I never said that I hated you. But yes, I am willing to invest in you. And as far as the mansion goes, yeah right. You gon' have to work your way up toward this kind of success. Ain't nothing free in this world, and it ain't sweet. Even if Phoenix did have the bread to put you up in a mansion like this, he would have to do it over my dead body. He belongs to me."

"Is that right?" Alicia stepped close enough to Natalia that her belly was rubbing against her arm.

"Yeah that's right, and don't you forget it." Natalia was ready to go to war over Phoenix. She was crazy about him and saw Alicia as a threat. The death of Phoenix Jr. was sure to bring Alicia and Phoenix together in a way that she was worried that she couldn't compete with. The busier she kept Alicia, and the further she made sure that Phoenix was away from Alicia, the better her mind would be eased.

"Well, check this out, Natalia. I don't want your man. I have no desire to be with Phoenix. We had a child together, and that was all there was to it. If you are willing to help me get on my feet, I will gladly accept your help, but you better know that I will pay you back in full."

Natalia snickered. "Aw, baby girl, it ain't even about the money. I mean, I'm gonna get what's mine, but I'm going to do this because it's imperative that we as sistahs help one another out. So you do what you have to, and I will as well. Pack your shit, because I promise to have you moved into a four bedroom house by the end of tomorrow, if not today." She looked her up and down. "And I would appreciate while you're staying under my roof that you would put some fuckin' clothes on. I can see through this, whatever this is, as if you aren't even wearing it."

She walked out of the room, and stopped. "Phoenix, wrap this shit up in here so we can talk about some business. Time is money." She left, walked down to their master bedroom, and closed the door.

Alicia waited for a second with her head down. She hated Natalia. She closed the guest bedroom door and made haste to Phoenix. She kissed his lips and licked all over them. Her hands were unbuckling his Chanel belt. She squeezed his dick.

"You finna fuck me right now while that abrasive ass bitch is down the hallway." She pulled her panties down just enough for him to see her trimmed pussy lips. She took his hand, and forced him to feel her heat. She pulled her panties down further until they were at the bottom over thighs.

Phoenix slid two fingers into her. He worked them in and out. Then pushed her toward the bed where he bent her over. "Gimme this shit, then." His dick was out and looking to find her crease.

Alicia bumped her ass back into him, and allowed for him to feel her heat. He slid deeply into her with one hard thrust.

She groaned, and crawled across the bed, leaving his dick shiny from her juices and jumping in the air. "I knew you still wanted me. You ain't over me yet, Phoenix."

Phoenix was stroking his piece in frustration. "Why are you playin' with me? Come here."

Alicia stood on her knees in the middle of the bed. "I know she got all of this money, and y'all got a special connection and all of that, but in the end, you're going to choose me. I'm one hunnit percent better than that bitch, and you know it."

She pulled up her panties and straightened her bra. Her fingers went through her shoulder length hair.

Phoenix fixed his clothes. "So that's what you're on, huh?" He laughed. "Awright, well we're gonna see about that." He fixed his belt, and flipped his piece upward so that the big head throbbed on top of his belt. He was still riled up. It had been a minute since he and Alicia had been active. He wanted to wax that ass.

Alicia scooted past him. "Yeah, I guess we'll see won't we?" She held the door open for him with a smirk on her face.

Phoenix eased into the hallway, feeling like he'd been played. "I got yo ass, though."

"I guess we finna see. Go tend to yo baby mama, Phoenix. Bye." She closed the door in his face.

Phoenix stood there for a second before he laughed to himself. "Yeah, I got her ass, watch."

Chapter 6

Smoke had been up for three days straight with minimal sleep. He had his closest dope boys, and the most successful trap houses around the city of Memphis, up and working just as hard. Money was his motivation, and he was pulling in large sums of it at a time, thanks to his undying hustler's ambition. Smoke had already made up his mind to take over the game in the South. He wanted Memphis to be the epicenter for everything, and he understood that in order to get there, he would have to pound the pavement, and destroy other cartels that were already formed, or were up and coming.

When the game all boiled down, it was about money, and power. Smoke knew that in order to possess power you needed to possess large sums of cash first. Cash that could be converted into digital numbers because it was twenty-twenty and nobody respected a hustler with all cash and no credit to show for it, or a certain number in the bank.

In order to graduate from an ordinary, everyday, run of the mill dope boy, a true hustler must possess money, both digital and cash in hand, power, respect, and artillery, which was hard to come by. You also needed an army of savages that didn't eat unless you fed them. Savages that were like pit bulls. Most pit bulls hated anything or anybody that wasn't its owner, and even at times, a vicious Pit bull hated its master as well, but it still remained loyal and protected its owner at all costs.

Smoke surrounded himself with starving, angry, cold blooded, loyal savages from Orange Mound. Most of the young killas that he'd grown up with, and when he saw their mothers, they knew his real name. Smoke didn't like other crews that were outside of Orange Mound, and he made sure that he put firing squads together that would take down any crew that he deemed an imminent, or up and coming threat.

51

The Game was all about supremacy, and the control of the drug flow. Whoever controlled the streets and its drug flow, controlled the city. Memphis was his homeland, and Smoke refused to allow for anybody else to control his city other than him.

It was a Friday night. There was light rain falling from the sky, and Smoke had Greedy riding in the passenger's seat, and Tyson in the back seat of his Lexus truck. He had a Mach .10 on his lap, and a blunt in his mouth. He took a pull from it, and blew the smoke to the roof of his truck. "Awright now, look, we're about two miles away from where we are set to meet Rivera. When we get here, I want you niggas to keep y'all eyes peeled. This is my first time fucking with dude, and even though he has a straight record in the slums, I don't put that much weight on that shit. If anything looks out of place, we lacing these mafuckas wit' no mercy. Y'all got that?"

Tyson surveyed the streets as they rolled down them. "Say, Smoke, how much money is in these bags by my feet?" Tyson kicked one of the two Gucci duffle bags. They were both heavy to the kick.

"A hundred thousand in every thang in each. One, fives, tens, twenties, fifties, and hunnits. Every thang. Why do you ask me that?"

"Because I'm just wondering why we would be doing business with somebody that we barely know, and taking so much money? Do you remember how it used to be when we were starving? Dawg, we would've tore a nigga's head for a hundred thousand dollars."

"By any means," Greedy said, with his finger over the trigger of his AK.

"Yeah, well now we the ones with the money, and we gotta be prepared for niggas like us. This Game is cold and cut throat. Life doesn't mean shit. A mafucka takes your life, and wipes your blood off of his weapon by the use of your cheek," Tyson explained.

"We know that, which is why we are playing no games. We gon' over here, and meet up with Rivera and see what these Choppas look like. And once again, I'ma say if anything looks out of place, we sweat the whole warehouse, period," Smoke reiterated.

"I got my troops en route in such a way. I don't trust that we might not be being followed, so I got my soldiers taking alternate routes, but the location is the same. By the time we get there and in place, it should be all good." Tyson was confident in his animals.

Greedy frowned. "Smoke, I'll blow my mother shit back for you, mane. Ya boy might be having those blue faces, but at the same time, that killa shit is still in me. Rivera will make the worst move of his life if he crosses us tonight. I don't give a fuck where these Mexicans from."

"Mexico City. They call themselves Chee-langos," Smoke said, popping a stick of him into his mouth. His breath tasted weird to him, and he didn't like that.

"Chee-langos, what the fuck is that?" Greedy wanted to know.

"It means that Rivera was born and raised in Mexico City. That's his homeland." Tyson answered the question for him. "Those Mexicans from Mexico City be racist as hell. I don't understand why they are even doing bidness wit' us black folk, but it looks like we're gonna have to trust you on this one, Smoke."

Smoke nodded, he felt a shiver go down his spine. "It's been a whole lot of warring between the Spanish Cartels over in Mexico. Mafuckas are dropping like flies, and all of them are trying to get a stranglehold of the United States, ever since

El Chapo went down. They were trying to kill his son and everything. However, Rivera's Cartel is supposed to be next up and coming when it comes to arms and weaponry. He heard about the Bread Gang, and they see that we are making noise through the state of Tennessee. The Mexican cartels are very racist. They only care about their own people, but even more than their people, they care about their money. They are great investors when it comes to the slums. This is why Rivera wanted to meet us, and close this deal. No matter their motive, ours is to get these weapons and to get out of New Mexico with our lives. I don't know much about this state, so we gotta be on point."

Greedy snickered. "On some real shit, I would love to blow one of those bitches' heads off. They are so short, and I remember when I was in the ninth grade, and visiting my cousins over in Los Angeles, like twenty of them bitches jumped on me. They fucked me up real good, too. I hated Mexicans ever since then."

"That sound like a dumb ass reason to hate a whole race of people, Greedy." Smoke shook his head in disgust.

"Never said I was perfect. I'm a killa, and I'm cool with that."

"Everybody be on point, we arrive in thirty minutes," Smoke ordered

***

Forty five minutes later, Smoke carried the two duffle bags full of cash into an aluminum plant and set them on the floor in front of him. He eyed the eight armed Mexican men in the room. Rivera stood in front. He was five feet five inches tall, with a bushy moustache, and pale skin. He was dressed in a tailor-made Italian suit. Smoke sized him up quickly. Every time he blinked his eyes, he saw himself putting bullet holes inside of Rivera.

Rivera walked over to the long wooden table that was in the middle of the warehouse. He slapped it with his hand. The sound resonated and echoed throughout the warehouse that was otherwise quiet. "Place the bag up here and allow me to count my money homie."

Smoke picked up the bags and placed them on the table. "At the same time you count this money, I need to be seeing what these Choppas you're offering to me feel like." He kept his hands on the handles of the bags.

Rivera mugged him. He looked over Smoke's shoulder at the armed Tyson, and Greedy. Greedy kept a mug on his face. He was hoping that things went south. If they did, he was already thinking about which of Rivera's men that he would hit first? He imagined the bloodshed and felt his penis hardening. Rivera snapped his fingers.

One of his men walked to the back of the twenty-twenty Lincoln Navigator, and pulled out a Mach Uzi. He handed it to Smoke. "This is a creation from Mexico."

Smoke held the street sweeper in his hand and took two steps back. "What the fuck is this?" It felt light in his hands. The barrel was long and narrow. The clip hanging out of the center was long as a table leg. There was a beam on top of it. The trigger was thin as a toothpick.

"That's a Mach combined with a Uzi. It's as precise as a Mach. 11, and spits rapidly and directly as a Uzi. It's less likely to jam, and it comes with its own cooling system. When the Mach Uzi gets to a certain degree, it becomes warm, and then cold all on its own. The cleaning is easy, and if you want to break it down, there are a series of connection buttons that releases certain parts of the weapon for dismantling. This is new to the military, and hasn't hit the streets just yet. Well until now that is." Rivera laughed. "The magazine holds a hundred rounds, but there are fifty round clips as well. The beam on top of it is easily rechargeable, and that's just that. The gun is eighty-five percent accurate from a hundred yards or less, more than that and the effective number drops considerably. So unless your prey is a fast sprinter, you should be good."

Smoke held the Choppa up, and looked through the scope. "I ain't planning on letting a mafucka get that far away before I kill his ass dead. What are we talking per weapon?"

"That depends on how close you plan on working with me, and I with you, for that matter. You see, the Sangre' Cartel is looking to fully invest within the Bread Gang. With us behind you, not only will you be a force, but we can help you to move out of Memphis, and into even richer cities where the need for your supply is high, and the resistance with us by your side will be low. I am talking about some major money."

"We're already making major money without any assistance from you boys down in Mexico. Why would I look to get involved with your Cartel when every single day I'm getting reports of how you muthafuckas are killing and chopping off the heads of your own? Everybody knows that you are all racists."

"My wife is from Veracruz. She is Afro Mexican. My children are of mixed blood. Any man that tells you that Rivera is a racist, I will chop his head off in front of you." He stepped into Smoke's face.

Greedy clutched his gun tight. "Say, mane, back yo ass up from my Potna. You're making me nervous."

Rivera eyed Greedy and nodded. He backed up. It would have been senseless to get into a major confrontation with Smoke's help. He had bigger fish to fry. "So, Smoke, listen to me. I respect you as a threat and a Drug Lord in the narcotics world. I see what you are doing in Memphis, and I know that you can do it throughout your community, in every city within the South, with us backing you. We can enter into this partnership and do what needs to be done. If we will, I will supply you with grade A artillery at fifty percent off. When it comes to the tar, you'll get top notch kilos from me for ten apiece. Not to mention, when it comes to the war, you will have our security backing."

"Why are you so thirsty for the Bread Gang to fuck wit you, Rivera? I need you to keep shit uncut for a moment." Smoke set the Mach Uzi on the table, and backed away from it.

"The black community needs to be run by black faces. It gives us longevity, and it keeps down the war and bloodshed. If a Mexican was to openly confess that he was running the black streets of Memphis, how many groups would gang up against us to get us out of their territories? How many in the Mexican communities would do the same if you were running their streets and they found out that you were?" Rivera asked.

"So you think that you're about to run shit through me, huh?" Smoke scoffed. "You must not have done your research on me, homeboy. I don't like honoring anybody except my boss. I am the boss. Now while it would be cool to have your Cartel looking over mine, I think I'ma have to pass. But what I will do is drop a bag for some of those Mach Uzis you were trying to sell me to begin with. Now what price are we talking?"

Rivera remained calm. "Smoke, I am coming to you before we invest in another cartel. If we do that, then you will become the enemy. I don't want this, and neither does anybody else in my outfit. But just like I understand the rules of the game, you must also."

Smoke placed a scowl on his face. "Aw, so you called me here for an ultimatum? You're basically saying that I can either roll with you, or be rolled over, huh?" He stepped closer to Rivera.

Rivera was not fazed by Smoke's moving forward. "That's exactly what I am saying in so many words."

Smoke looked him up and down. "One thang I have never been afraid of is a little war, Rivera. If you thanking it's sweet, then come and fuck wit the gang. I'm letting you know right now, though, that your ass is about to be sadly muthafuckin' mistaken."

"To show you that I mean business I have already brought along ten of the Mach Uzis that I was going to sell to you. They are yours for free." He snapped his fingers again.

The same henchmen from before came and placed a chest before Smoke, and then backed away from him. "They are all there."

Smoke opened the chest, and saw that it was filled with the Mach Uzis. He looked up to Rivera. "I brought a hunnit K, that's what I'ma leave you with. The Bread Gang don't take no handouts. Never have, and we never will. We get everything out of the mud."

"Until now. Vamanos." Rivera twirled his right hand into a circle. His crew rushed into the Navigator. Seconds later they were peeling away without another word.

"Muthafuckas." Smoke was confused. He watched the Navigator disappear out of the warehouse. He stood still for a few moments before he and his crew packed up both the money and guns and left.

Chapter 7

Sabrina ran her fingers through her thick, curly hair while she looked over the bow of the yacht that Kevin rented for the weekend. She took a deep breath and inhaled the scent of the salt coming off of the blue water. The sun shined brightly overhead. Big seagulls squawked as they flew over the Yacht. Sabrina hoped that neither of the birds dropped shit on the boat.

Kevin came behind her and wrapped his arms around her waist. He was five feet ten inches tall, biracial, black and white, light skinned, with a bald head, and a stocky frame. He kissed her neck. "It feels like I just met you a week ago, Sabrina, and not six months. I can still remember how you looked sitting all alone in the back booth of Aunt Nikki's restaurant, with your eye glasses on, tapping away on your laptop. I thought you were the finest woman I had ever laid eyes on, and I still do, to this day."

Sabrina smiled. "Oh, you still think so, huh?"

"You damn right I do." He held her more firmly. "Four of my five artists won Grammys last night. Four out of five. The internet is already buzzing, and our social media accounts are going haywire. Success is coming fast and steady, yet I still feel so incomplete. You wanna know why that is?"

Sabrina turned around so that she was facing him. "Why is that?" She picked a strand of her long curly hair off of her face.

"Because you aren't my wife, and you should be." He searched her eyes with his light brown ones.

"Wife, Kevin we barely know each other." She eased out of his embrace. "We're barely past friends." She stepped to the railing of the boat and watched the sun begin to slowly descend behind the clouds.

"Sabrina, when you're forty-six years old, knowing a person a week seems like a lifetime, especially when you're being pulled into a hundred different directions. I have been with you now, consistently, for four months straight. We dated for two months, or slightly less than two. Baby, what I am saying is that I am about to enter into a new phase of fans and fortune. I don't want to experience any of it without you."

He slid his hand into his pocket, and pulled out the ring box that contained a two carat diamond engagement ring. He held it in his right hand and took a hold of hers with his left. He lowered himself to his right knee. "Sabrina, I love you. I want to give you the world, one day at a time. I know that I am not the most handsome man in the world, or the most perfect, but I promise to work hard every single day to make and keep you happy. Since you have been a part of my life, things have gotten progressively better. I am asking you, Sabrina Stevens, if you will be my wife?" He popped open the box. The ring glistened in the sunlight.

Sabrina was stuck for a moment. The only person she could think of was Phoenix. She looked down at Kevin's face and felt lost. "Kevin, this is so sudden. I swear, I had no idea."

"So does that mean that you will be my wife?" He held the ring up for her to marvel.

"What about Kandace? You two are still married." Sabrina was looking to buy time.

"The divorce has been finalized. As of today, I am a free man."

Sabrina bit on her finger nails. She felt like she was going to become hysterical if she didn't get a hold of herself. She closed her eyes and took a deep breath. "You know what, Kevin? Yes, yes, I will marry you, baby."

Kevin represented stability, and long-term security. *How could she go wrong?* She thought. She deserved a lavish life.

Her life had been rough enough and full of struggles already. Kevin would fill in the blanks where she needed help. She was sure of it.

"Yeah?" Kevin was excited.

"Yeah." She exclaimed.

Kevin slid the ring onto her ring finger, stood up and kissed her lips. "I promise, baby. I'm about to make you so happy." He kissed her over and over.

Sabrina smiled. "I know, Kevin. I promise, I know."

***

Phoenix sat clenching and unclenching his fingers. He was highly upset and irritated. "So you told this nigga that you would marry him before you even hollered at me?" He was trying his best to remain calm.

Sabrina stood in the living room of her apartment. She was nervous and starting to feel like she had made the wrong decision. "Phoenix, why do I have to run all of my decisions by you before I make them?"

He ignored her question. "Why did you tell this muthafucka that you would marry him? Huh? Explain this shit to me right now, Sabrina, because I am this close to fucking you up." He held his fingers in the sign of a pinch.

Shante looked on fearful. "Daddy, should I go to the back room until you and cousin Sabrina are done talking?" she asked, holding her iPad in her right hand.

"Yeah, gon' back there lil' mama and do your own thing. Me and Sabrina need to hash a few things out." Phoenix ordered his daughter.

"Okay." Shante lowered her head and slowly walked down the hallway until she got to Sabina's room, and closed the door.

"Back to you. Explain yourself."

Sabrina shook her head. "Phoenix, you ain't my daddy. I don't have to explain nothin' to you. I told the man that I will marry him, and that is that." She walked past him into the kitchen.

Phoenix was behind her before she could make it to the refrigerator. He grabbed a handful of her hair. She shrieked. He tightened his grip. "Sabrina, you think that shit is a game, huh?" He pulled her out of the kitchen and back into the living room where he sat on the couch. He pulled her over his lap and trapped her legs. He yanked up her skirt exposing her ice blue thongs that separated her cheeks. He gripped each cheek and rubbed them, warming them up for what he was getting ready to do.

"Bitch, I swear to God, if you don't tell me why you chose to marry this man, I'm about to beat the yellow off of your lil' thick ass." He smacked her hard on her backside, causing her cheeks to jiggle. "What the fuck you tell him yeah for?"

Sabrina screamed, and groaned. The slap hurt her. "He loves me, Phoenix, and he's rich. I know this man will take care of me for the rest of my life."

"So you're marrying him for money?" He was furious. He rubbed all over her ass and slapped it hard. Once, then twice, and then four times in a row. Then he was rubbing all over it, and in between her crack. He stuffed her panties further into her crease. "Are you marrying him for his money?"

"I don't know. Stop. Stop. I don't know." She tried to break out of his embrace.

Phoenix held her tighter. Smack. Smack. Smack. Smack. He went to town on that ass. "You. Got. This. Nigga. Thinking. You. Bout. To. Be. His. Wife?" Smack. Smack. Smack. Smack.

Sabrina squeezed her ass cheeks as tight as she could to prevent the pain that she was feeling. She bit into his side. She could feel his hard penis poking against her. "I'm sorry, Phoenix. I'm sorry. Damn."

Smack. Smack. Smack. Smack.

She kicked her legs wildly. "Please."

Phoenix ignored her pleas. He spanked her for five straight minutes before he flipped her off of him. "Get yo ass off of me."

Sabrina fell to the ground, rubbing her backside. "Why you do that?"

Phoenix picked her up and sat her on the couch. He reached between her thighs and yanked her panties off of her with one vicious tug. He got to his knees, and stuffed his face in her gap, eating hungrily. His tongue was a blur as it went in and out of her pussy. Then he was sucking both sex lips at the same time, before he opened them and began twirling his tongue around her clitoris.

After the spanking Sabrina was soaking wet. She felt taken advantage of. She felt disciplined. She felt degraded. She moaned and bucked forward. "Phoenix, I'm sorry. I ain't gon' marry him. I promise."

Phoenix pushed her knees to her breasts, and stood up. He pulled out his piece and slid into her in one motion. His back began to pop at full speed. "Marry who? Marry who? You my mafuckin' cuz. Mine." His pounding became relentless.

Sabrina closed her eyes, and came hard. She tried to take her legs down, and came again, harder than the first time. She began to whimper. Phoenix was tearing that pussy up with no remorse. "Unn. Unn. Phoenix. You're killing me. You're killing me. Aww fuck." She came again shivering as if she were out in the freezing cold.

Phoenix bit into his bottom lip, and pulled out as he began to cum. "Suck dis mafucka, cuz. Hurry up."

Sabrina took a hold of his piece and sucked him into her mouth. She sucked him fast, and pumped it at the same time as he began to cum hard again and again. She gagged, and kept sucking. She popped him out and kissed all over his piece.

"I'm sorry, Phoenix." More sucking. "I didn't know what I was saying to him." More sucking. She popped him back out. "I swear to God, I won't marry him. I promise."

She closed her eyes and sucked Phoenix while he ran his fingers through her hair. When she opened them she saw Shante in the middle of the hallway watching them. She tried to pull her mouth off of Phoenix's piece to tell him, but Phoenix grabbed her head and forced her to stay sucking on him until he came ten minutes later. By that time Shante had slowly left the hallway two minutes prior.

***

"So you gon tell me why you went so crazy after I told you that I was going to marry Kevin?" Sabrina asked as she placed her thick thigh over Phoenix's form. They were laying up in her bed after a shower where Phoenix had fucked her again from the back while he spanked her. She'd moaned so loud that she was sure that Shante had heard her, but she didn't care.

"Because you belong to me. I don't even know this Kevin ass nigga. We have really been through it together ever since we were kids, and you are the closest person that I have to Kamya." Kamya was Sabrina's sister, and one of the loves of Phoenix's young life.

"So you saying that you only give a fuck because I remind you of Kamya? That doesn't make me feel good." She sat up, and placed her back against the headboard.

Phoenix kissed her inner thigh. "You're bugging. What I'm saying is that we are family, and we belong to each other. Fuck Kevin. He can't do shit for you that I can't do. Not one thing."

"You're so possessive of me, Phoenix, that's so funny. It's crazy, too, because to be real with you, I like that." She slid back down in the bed. "You know damn well that I don't care about this man like that. Why wouldn't you allow me to use him for his money so that we can have another outlet in this world? It ain't like we have to stop doing what we do. You already know that ain't happening." She took a hold of his piece and sucked it for two minutes, before sliding on to his waist and easing down on it. She moaned and closed her eyes. She slowly began to ride him.

Phoenix held her ass. "Damn, this family pussy." He closed his eyes, and opened them. "We're going to figure this shit out then. Fuck. If he... Holding. Like. You say." He laid back while Sabrina rode him picking up speed. "We gon'. Get. His. Ass."

"Okay. Uhh. Shit. Shante saw us." She sped up the pace. "She saw us fucking. Aw shit. She watched the whole thing." She began to ride him so fast that Phoenix had to hold her ass before she fell off of him.

"What. How?"

Sabrina bit into his neck and came to imagine that she was Shante and watching Phoenix screw her. "You need to talk to your daughter, Phoenix. We might've screwed her up." She said coming to a halt, shivering on top of him.

"Damn, what do I say?" He asked, disbelieving that Shante had caught them in the act.

"I don't know, but you better figure it out. She is the same age that we were when we started doing our thing so..."

"Yeah, I got it." But he didn't know if he would actually have it. He felt embarrassed already.

The more and more he thought about it, he began to curse himself for being so reckless. He would have to find a way to sit Shante down, and pray that she wasn't scarred from what she'd witnessed. He sighed and felt sick. "Damn, you're always getting me in trouble."

"Me?"

"Yeah you." And then he fell back and allowed for his mind to race like crazy.

Chapter 8

Smoke sat on the couch counting a twenty thousand dollar stack that Tyson had only ten minutes ago dropped off to him. He licked his thumb and kept counting while the sounds of his newly signed rap group under Bread Gang spit through the speakers of his phone. He nodded his head and could understand why the streets of Memphis were calling the click the truth, and why Tyson was going so hard to keep money behind the group. Smoke especially liked one of the main rappers who kept his attention while he spit and had cerebral dope boy punch lines. Yeah, he would continue to invest in them. Legal money was the ultimate goal, he thought.

There were three knocks on the front door. Smoke made his way to it and looked out of the peephole. Precious stood in front of it with her lips full of gloss. They shimmered. He stepped back and laughed, then pulled the door open. "What it is, shawty?"

"I'm here. I know you probably thought I was scared to come, but I'm here." She stepped into the apartment, smelling good, and rocking a Fendi dress that clung to her curves like a second skin. Smoke's eyes immediately went to that ass that was jiggling like Jello with each step that she took. The dress fell just below the swell of her apple bottom. Her thick thighs were on display, lovely.

Smoke closed the door. He held the wads of cash in each hand. He already knew how the game went when you were trying to flex on a bitch because you saw future potential in her, which is what he saw in Precious. "Shawty, did you get permission from your parents before they let you come over here?"

"Ha, ha, ha." She looked around the apartment. "Are you really the Smoke that I've been hearing so much about?"

"Ain't another mafucka name ringing louder than mine in Memphis, so you already know what it is."

She scoffed. "I'm just saying that because this apartment ain't really all that, playboy. A lot of the shit you got, we got at home, and we broke. Can't say that I'm impressed." She couldn't help but to be blunt. "They were making it seem like you were this major baller, and you had Memphis on lock. Talking about you're a legend, like Taurus, and all of that stuff."

Smoke shrugged his shoulders. "I ain't reached that Taurus status yet, but I'll be there real soon if I keep handling my bidness the way that I am. Besides it's twenty-twenty, I am my own legend. I ain't chasing no nigga." He looked her over as she sized up his entertainment system. "Sit yo ass down anyway, ain't nobody tell you to walk around my shit appraising my crib."

"Sound like I struck a nerve." She sat on the couch and crossed her thick thighs. She pulled the hem of her dress down. She could sense that she was showing too much skin.

"When you a boss, a bitch can't strike no nerve unless she's affecting your paper in a negative way. Since I ain't got no stakes in yo ass, you ain't did shit."

Precious ran her tongue over her upper row of teeth. "When a man's ego is as big as yours, and you don't acknowledge what he's trying to flex with right before your eyes, it bruises him. It looks to me like I've bruised you, but you'll be awright." She pulled a blunt from her Fendi purse. "I got that Kush, what's good?"

Smoke held the money in one big handful and tossed her a lighter. "Spark that shit and let me see what you are blowing." He sat across from her and eyed her young thighs. Because of his constant grind, it had been a few days since he'd been able to get a shot of pussy. And all while hustling over the last past week, the only person he could think about was Precious. Her body was so righteous, and she was so off limits, which upped her stake, in his opinion.

Precious took two pulls off of her blunt and passed it over to him. Leaning forward, Smoke saw a nice portion of her breasts, nearly to the darkness of her areolas. "So tell me, Smoke, why you ain't got a bunch of project bitches walking around here half naked right now, like every other trap house in Memphis?"

Smoke sat the money on his lap and snickered. "You've been in every other trap house in Memphis already?"

She glared at him. "You know what I mean?"

Smoke took four quick pulls of the Ganja and held it. He passed the blunt back to Precious. The smoke irritated his throat. It made his chest burn. He could feel the high come over him before he released the fumes into the air. He was lifted. "I can have that shit if I want it, but that shit doesn't intrigue me no more. I'm on some other shit. It's all about this bread." He gathered it back up and placed it on the table in front of her. He made sure that he'd put all of the hundred dollar bills in the front so she could see it.

Precious peeped him, and once again she wasn't impressed. "I come from a whole line of boss women. They raised me in this mind frame that if a nigga like you is showing me his money without spending it on me, he ain't nothing but a front, and my target should be his pride, and the money will follow. You're supposed to be this boss of a nigga, and you're sitting there acting like some common dope boy. Bosses don't need to flash their money. The streets have already spoken of their worth. The fact that you are flashing that ten thousand dollars let's me know that you ain't been a boss for long."

"It's twenty thousand, and I've been a boss my whole life." Smoke felt irritated. He couldn't believe that he was allowing Precious to get to him in the way that she was.

"What's so crazy is that I didn't even have to count your money. You told me how much you were holding all on your own. Suppose somebody had sent me at yo' ass. I would have a nice bit to report, and broke as these niggas is in Memphis, they a come at yo ass over twenty gees, boy, and you know it." She took a few more puffs of the blunt and passed it back to him.

Smoke eyed her closely. "What's good wit' you?"

"What do you mean?" She batted her eyelashes at him.

"You ain't stopped running your mouth since you got here. You talking this shit like you really in the mud. Bitch, what's the reason you came out to fuck wit a nigga tonight?" Smoke sat the blunt in the ashtray.

"I just heard a lot about you. You told me that if I wanted to fuck with you, then to hit you up on Facebook, which is what I did. You invited me over, and now I'm here. So I guess the real question is why did you invite me over?"

"To fuck that young ass pussy. That's why." Smoke was done playing games. If Precious wanted to act like she was deep in the trenches, then it was time to take the gloves off.

"Oh really?"

He scooted to the edge of the couch. "Bring yo' yella ass here."

"Is that anyway for you to talk to a woman?" She remained seated.

"Good thing you ain't no woman yet. Get yo ass over here. Bitch, now."

Precious jerked her head back and awaited before she stood up. Now she was nervous. "Over there?"

"Over here."

70

She set her purse on the couch and walked over to him. She was slightly pigeon toed. When she got to him, she stood directly in front of him. "What's up?"

Smoke looked into her eyes and smiled evilly. He trailed his eyes cowardly over her gorgeous body. His right hand gripped her ass, then he was rubbing the whole backside with both hands. She was thick. Her flesh was hot. He could feel it through her clothes. "Why you stop all that talking now?"

"I'm just trying to see what you're up to? I mean, plus, I said all I had to say."

Smoke trailed his hand between her thighs, and up them until his fingers was rubbing against the crotch of her panties. "How many trap niggas you done let hit this pussy?" He trailed his hand backward until he was cuffing her hot ass cheeks.

"It ain't sweet, can't just no anybody have some of my body."

"Bitch, that ain't no answer. How many?"

She smacked his hand away. "Don't worry about it. It ain't none of your business." She walked away from him, sat back on the couch, and crossed her thighs. She neglected to pull the dress down this time. Smoke could see her white panties through the crux of her thighs.

He stood up. "The reason I'm asking is because I can't be seen wit no dog hoes, or no lil' bitches that every nigga in Memphis done ran through. If you wanna be in the passenger seat of the Rafe, then you gotta be a bad bitch, and you gotta be untapped by these regular ass niggas. It's as simple as that. So how many dope boys you done fucked in the Mound?"

"None. It ain't not one nigga in Memphis who can say that he fucked me. I'm willing to bet whatever you wanna bet on that, too."

Smoke came over and squatted beside her. He placed his hand on her right thigh. "You mean to tell me that you're walking around all strapped like this, and ain't none of these niggas hit?"

"That's exactly what I'm telling you." She looked into his eyes with her green ones.

Smoke looked down at her thighs and began to rub them. "We are about to change all of that. If ain't no other nigga hit, then I'm about to be the first, and I don't give a fuck how childish that shit sound." He slid his hand in between her thighs, and smushed her sex lips together through her panties. "Open yo' legs a lil' bit for me."

She closed them tighter and pulled his hand from between her thighs. "I don't know what you think dis is, potna, but you have to come mo' correct den dat. You sitting hurr wit' all dis cash and you ain't said shit about checking none of it to me while you're touching all on me and shit." She stood up and grabbed her purse.

Smoke got up. "Aw so you want a mafucka to pay for the pussy. That's what you on?"

"I'm trying to get my hands on a bag, a steady bag, might I add. Now you got all of these strip clubs, trap houses, and pill spots, but you ain't said how you're finna benefit me. You start talking about how you gon' do that, and we can talk about how you gon' get some of dis fresh na na." She raised the dress so that the bottom hint of her panties showed from the front. "You know you want dis lil kitten, too."

Damn, she was driving him crazy. Smoke had never felt like taking some pussy before, but Precious was driving him insane. "Aiight den, shawty, let's talk about it. What you wanna do?"

"I wanna move some of those pill thangs, and when I hit eighteen, I wanna do my thing in one of your strip clubs so I can really get my bag up. I don't want to dance though, even though I can, I wanna be a bartender, or a bottle girl."

Smoke imagined her in that role, and he nodded his head. She would be a money maker. He was sure of that. "Awright, lil' one. And what else?"

"I come from nothin'. I ain't trying to be broke my whole life. If I'm messing with you on this intimate level, I need you to help me level all the way up. I need to check a bag on a regular so I can help my people conquer their struggles. If you can help me do that, I'll be your lil' young slut. Whatever you say will go. You can have me and my friend." She blushed.

"Yo friend, where is she at?" Smoke was intrigued.

"Aw, you'll meet her in time. But for now, do we have an understanding?"

Smoke nodded. "I understand the struggle, shawty, and I know what you on. Money ain't got gender. If you wanna chase this paper, I'ma help you get as much of it as you can, because the more you get, the more I will ultimately be getting. So I'm wit' you. Now as far as this body goes." He pulled her to him and gripped that ass. He cuffed the cheeks and pulled the dress up. "When you gon let me fuck this lil' pussy?" His hand dipped under, and inside of her thing from the back. He found her lips and played with the skin of them before trying to find her entrance.

She pushed him backward. "When you help me get some type of green, I'ma give you what you really want. That's my word." She removed his hands from her ass and pulled her dress down. "You got all of my information, Smoke, when you're really ready, make sure you hit me up." She opened the door to his apartment and left.

Smoke stood in the middle of the living room erect and irritated. "Damn, this lil bitch." He glanced down to the money on the table and was thinking about grabbing a bundle of it and giving it to Precious, just so he could hit the kitty, when Tyson stuck his head in the door.

"Bruh, we have a problem. Greedy needs our assistance like right now. Mafuckas just murdered three of the guys."

Chapter 9

"It took you a long time to finally get up with me, Phoenix, usually I don't have so much patience." Kilroy took a sip of his champagne and adjusted the headphones that were on his head as he looked out of the helicopter that both he and Phoenix were flying in over the city of Philadelphia, Pennsylvania.

"You told me to get my ducks in a row before I came to fuck wit' you, and that's what I did. All of that hot shit in Tennessee that was done ain't forgotten about by the authorities, but at least I was able to put a few Band-Aids over some of the bleeding if you get my drift."

Kilroy grunted that he did. He was bald, heavy set, and dark skinned, with a mouth full of gold. The trenches of Philly revered him as a black god. "Yo, kid, you already know that I had to extend my hand as best I could from afar. I got a senator for your state on board and hit a judge to make that shit temporarily go away. But it's just like you said though, it's only a Band-Aid. In this game it's all about the money. As long as you are willing to pay for your freedom, it will last a long time. But the minute you stop greasing palms is the same instant that you will be living in a prison cell. That's just the way the game goes, Dunn." He sipped from his bottle again. "But it's good that you finally reached out to a nigga, now is critical, especially since you removed yourself from the situation down south."

"That shit ain't dead, though. I'm just giving myself some time, and the state of Tennessee some time away from me. There is still a nice amount of unfinished business that I gotta squash before it's all said and done." Phoenix took two pulls from his blunt, as he felt a migraine pound behind his eyes. "Now, the reason I hit you up is because, as you can see, I'm down in Florida now, but I'm still fucking with a few states on this hustle shit, Tennessee being one of them, and I need that plug on the girly, and on the boy-boy." In the game, girly meant cocaine, and boy-boy was heroin.

Kilroy mugged him. "Nigga, I heard that your woman is one of the deepest Queenpins in the game. Natalia's name rings all the way here in Philly, back out west to California, and all over the south. How the fuck is you looking for a plug, and she is the plug? That don't make no sense to me."

"When I started fucking with Natalia, it wasn't because I needed her to support me. I'm my own man. I was in the game before she came into my life, and I wanna continue to operate inside of it on my own. I was born for this shit. So what's good?"

"What's good is that you sound like a damn fool. Pride always comes before the fall, Phoenix. You're sitting here in a helicopter with me, trying to establish a secure plug, when I am telling you that your woman and her people are my plug. We fuck wit that Rebirth out here, kid, and it got them fiends nodding like they watching a boring ass movie or somethin'. The kilos go for dirt cheap, and I'm making a five hundred percent profit off of each batch. Natalia got shit on lock. You're fucking her, but at the same time, your pride is fucking you. That's unfortunate." He shook his head.

Phoenix became angry. "So what are you saying, Kilroy?"

"I'm saying that there is nothing that I can do for you that your woman can't. Nigga, you plugged. Shit, I thought you were getting in touch with me because you wanted to put me on more than I already am. Then when you got to hollering this shit, it threw me all of the way off. But listen to me, take yo ass back to Miami and lock that shit down with Natalia. Once you do that, I'ma need you as a plug, because me and my Rotten To The Core Mafia just moved into New York and Boston with this Rebirth, and we taking shit over. The war is minimal, and the money is plentiful. If I can get a steady, stronger plug on the Rebirth, then we can really affect some shit. It's twenty-twenty, the election is this year, and I am looking to see if I can get my person into the White House. If I can do that, the sky's the limit." Kilroy drank from his bottle.

Phoenix's mind was blown. There he was thinking about having Kilroy become his plug, when, like Kilroy said, he was already sleeping with the number one plug in the United States and he didn't even recognize it. Second to that, Kilroy was thinking of buying a president with Natalia as his plug, and Phoenix couldn't see outside of his ghetto frame of thinking. Though he had a nice amount of money saved up, mentally, he was nothing more than a regular dope boy in the slums, and that was sad to him. He needed to open up his mind and expand himself more.

***

That night, he held Natalia in his arms in front of the fireplace of their mansion. It was ten o'clock, and both seemed to have so much on their minds that neither spoke for a full thirty minutes before Natalia broke the silence.

"Would I be wrong if I wanted to name our son after you?" She continued to watch the wood crackle and pop inside of the fireplace.

"What made you ask that question?" Phoenix rubbed her belly. She was shirtless, and her belly was poked out, ready to burst.

"Because I feel like every man wants his first son to be named after him. It's sort of like a rite of passage. But would I be wrong if I did, considering the circumstances of your last son, and Alicia, for that matter?"

"First of all it's not just on you to name him, it's a us thing. Secondly, I think that would cause a whole lot of controversy. Alicia would feel some type of way, and who's to say by us doing that, it wouldn't curse him to suffer the same fate as Junior?"

"I don't really care how it would make Alicia feel. That ain't my problem, it's yours. But as far as that last part goes, do you really think that our child would be cursed just because of his name?"

Phoenix shrugged his shoulders. "I hope not, but I'm slightly superstitious. You know how we are in the South."

"Yeah, stupid." She rolled her eyes.

"I guess."

"It's all good, then, I'm naming him after his grandfather that I never got the chance to meet. Did you know that I've never even seen my father's grave? How ridiculous is that?"

"He died in prison. Don't they keep the body in there or something?" Phoenix was unsure. He pulled out his cellphone and Googled it.

"I don't know what they do, but the staff said they cremated him. Nobody in the family has his ashes, either. I find that kind peculiar, don't you?"

"It says here that prisoners are buried in a regular graveyard, right along with everybody else. Some states bury them shackled, while others bury them regularly. I don't see anything here about cremation, and my father always told me that Taurus was buried in Texas. I never heard anything about cremation."

"Yeah, well that's what my mother told me, but she could be wrong. She was never right about much anyway." Natalia sighed. "I wanna name our son after my father. You can give him the middle name, and he'll have your last name, of course.

I'm assuming that we will be switching mine over to Stevens as well, soon, right?"

Phoenix kept rubbing her belly. "Shawty, I know you ain't talking that shit that I thank you is?"

"Yeah, why not?" She turned around so that she was facing him. "We're fucking already. I'm having your child, and we live together. Phoenix, how much weirder do you think things can really get?" She raised her left eye brow.

Phoenix stared at her for a moment. The reflection of the fire danced over her skin. He slowly slid back and stood up. "What would getting married solve, Natalia? Damn, we already live in sin like a muthafucka."

Natalia held her stomach and managed to climb to her feet, with his help. She smacked his hand away. "You're worried about sin, Phoenix? Come on now. If anybody is close to Satan, it's you." She rolled her eyes. "And yes, I wanna get married. I deserve to be a wife. Since I'm in love with you, then it should be you that is my husband. It's pure and simple."

Phoenix shook his head. "I ain't marrying no bitch. Fuck that. That marriage shit is a joke anyway. It's only a ploy for the government to be all up in your business for nothin'. It makes no sense."

Natalia stood with her head down. "I'm sorry. Did you just call me a bitch, and lump me into the same category with all of those other trifling ass Americans that you've been fucking on?"

"You know what I mean, Natalia. Look, I ain't marrying you. You my wifey, and that's enough for me."

"Well, it's not enough for me. The only time men get to calling women their wifey instead of their wife is when they are trying to buy time. More often than not, a wifey is merely a place holder for a wife that a man will find while he's stringing her stupid ass along."

"Natalia, let's talk about anything else. This marriage shit ain't happening."

"Oh, it ain't happening because you say it ain't? That's how this shit goes now?" She ran her fingers through her hair that dropped past her ass. She was frustrated and felt like attacking Phoenix.

"It ain't happening. That shit ain't even legal. You are my cousin, Natalia. Is that shit not clicking in your brain?" He tapped on his temple. "They will book our ass."

"Only in America. I got a jet. We can fly to any other country to make it happen. But then again, it ain't about that. Is it, Phoenix? N'all, it ain't. It's about yo black ass being scared of a fuckin' commitment. You can hit the pussy, and do the forbidden thing behind closed doors, but when it all boils down, you ain't about a commitment. This is why you left Alicia hanging, Kamya, and now me. It's fuckin' ridiculous." She stormed out of the living room and into the kitchen. Her mouth was dry. She opened a bottle of orange juice and began to drink it.

Phoenix was stuck. "When it comes to you bitches, I don't understand why shit just can't flow naturally. When we are chilling, man, let's chill. We wanna fuck, let's fuck. Why do y'all insist on putting a label on everything? Please explain to me why we need to be married in order for us to love each other. Explain that dumb ass shit, Natalia."

"Phoenix, if you call me a bitch again, I am going to cut you. Did you forget that I am black and Russian? My temper is ridiculous, and my emotions are all over the place. Now respect me, and don't call me a bitch again. You do." She pulled a butcher's knife out of the knife holder. "And I swear on our child that I will stab you tonight."

Phoenix exhaled loudly. "Please answer my question?"

"Phoenix, marriage is important to me. That's all you need to know. I am ready to be a wife and a mother. The two are supposed to go hand in hand. If you want me to be happy, you would make me a wife. If you want to see me scorned, then make me a statistic, and see which will fare better for you and our family. That's all I got to say. Good night." She slammed the half empty juice on the table. "I need some space, so don't come fuckin' wit me tonight." She disappeared down the long hall before she slammed the bedroom door.

"It's always something with these hoes, man. Always." Phoenix punched his fist. "Marriage, really?" He flopped on the couch and lowered his head in depression.

Shante wandered out of her room, and into the living room, where she sat on his lap. She wrapped her arm around his neck and kissed his cheek. "I love you, daddy. I know you are stressed out right now, but just know that your baby girl loves you." She kissed him again and hugged him tight.

Phoenix held her with his lips pressed to the side of her forehead. He melted. His anger subsided. The words from Shante's mouth had been all that he needed to hear to clear his mind. He stood up and walked around the living room with her for a moment. "Baby, do you wanna talk about what you saw between me and Sabrina the other night?"

Shante tightened her arms and legs around his body. She hid her face into his neck. "Daddy, I'm in the sixth grade. I know what y'all was doing, and no, I don't wanna talk about it right now."

He held her and laughed. "Okay, baby, but whenever you are ready, you let daddy know." He kissed her cheek.

Shante nodded. "Okay, daddy. Can you just hold me for a moment before you put me down?"

"I got you." He held her for a full hour, while she clung to him happily.

Chapter 10

Greedy adjusted the passenger's seat of the stolen Buick Park Avenue and slammed a magazine into the Mach Uzi he held on his lap. Half of his face was covered by a black ski mask, and he wore black leather gloves over his hands. He was hyped up off of four Percocet sixties, and a gram of the Rebirth. His eyes were low, and he was red hot with anger.

Smoke looked over at him. "Lil' homie, you awright over there?"

Greedy shook his head. "You know how I am when it comes to the homeland, Smoke. I don't like no nigga flexing on the Mound like they do shit harder than us, and I most definitely can't stand for a mafucka to come through our hood dropping bodies. They kilt four of my lil' homies yesterday, and you already know I can't let that shit ride, so I wanna go in here and make a splash."

"I still thank it's too early to be retaliating against these West Memphis niggas, bruh. Dis shit just happened last night. It ain't even been twenty-four hours yet. Who's to say that they ain't waiting on us to retaliate, or the police ain't loafing on us."

"I don't give a fuck about none of that. If these niggas ready, then we are about to get it in? If twelve is lurking, then they can catch these mafuckas, too. These bullets don't discriminate. I ain't about to let these fuck niggas drop four of us and we don't do shit about it."

"Greedy, how you know it's these West Memphis boys anyway?" Smoke asked, looking over at him.

"One of the lil' homies that got smoked was telling me that these fools were talking about rolling through the area and dropping somethin' for a few weeks now, because two of theirs got popped up in front of that old school sistah, Nell's, dro spot. I really ain't put no weight to it because I thought mafuckas wasn't stupid enough to actually come at the Mound, but I guess ignorance come in all fashions, cause I'm definitely on some ignorant shit right now."

"Smoke, we got that bag now, big homie. Tell me why we finna get our own hands dirty when we can drop a bag on a nigga head and keep it moving?" Tyson asked, feeling like this was a stupid mission for them to be going on. Sometimes Greedy really irked his nerves.

"Because we are born and bred by Orange Mound. If a mafucka killed somebody where we come from, it's only right that we go handle our bidness first hand. Lil' homie nem wasn't no older than sixteen. That's four funerals that I gotta pay for because this is my section. Funerals running every bit of fifteen to twenty thousand a piece. That's the hit money right there. You feel me on that?"

"Hell yeah, I do. I guess I didn't even think about it like that until you just told me all of that. Damn, bruh." Tyson was lost for words.

"Yeah, plus we don't need to be getting all soft just because we got that bag. If mafuckas get to looking at us like we're prey, then we are going to be in some serious trouble, especially with Smoke opening up all of these businesses around Memphis. All of dem bitches gone be targets after a while."

"Now you're using your head, Greedy. Sometimes I forget if you even have that mafucka." Smoke laughed at him, but Greedy kept his eyes focused on one road. "Who is supposed to be calling for these boys anyway?"

"Some fool named Pappy. He got a lil' team of savages that roll under him and they all are ready to pop that gun. I don't think that they are armed with much, though. About a

month back, Orange sold them like twenty burner hand pistols." Greedy looked over his shoulder at Tyson. "You ain't
heard about them having shit else did you?"

"Nall, and I kept my ear to the street, too. The only mafuckas that have been getting rid of pistols is us. After Black
Haven and Mikey got hit up, they were trying to recover as
best as they could, so they needed all of the guns that they
could get. I don't think these niggas really on shit, though.
Let's just roll over here and handle bidness and get the fuck
back. My Bread Gang rappers need me on side of them. How
the fuck am I going to be their manager, if I'm always on some
dumb shit like this?"

Greedy mugged Tyson. "Aw, so you think handling bidness for my lil homies is dumb? What, cause they ain't rapping
like yo lil' crew, they don't mean shit?" Greedy was heating
up.

"I didn't mean it like that. I'm just saying that I got mil-
lionaire squad goals, and it's impossible for me to chase a bag
if I'm always being involved on some stupid shit like this. I
mean, I ain't no lil' nigga like y'all. I got a fifteen year old
daughter that I gotta take care of. Eliza depends on me. I'm all
she got."

"Oh, so now we are throwing our kids in the mix as a reason for why we shouldn't be riding for my lil' homies? Man,
fuck that theory, and fuck you, Tyson, if you ain't bout that
life no more. Matter of fact, we don't even need you. Me and
the homie can handle this bidness by ourselves. It won't be the
first time that the heat was on and yo ass ducked out on us."
Greedy snapped.

"Y'all chill that shit out. It's always been us, and that's
how it's going to stay. Tyson, this bidness ain't gon take that
long. As soon as we done, you can jump back on tour with
your crew like none of this ever happened."

"Nigga, I don't need you. On some real shit, it feels like you getting soft to me. A mafucka gets a few coins in his pocket and all of the sudden he ain't bout that life no more. I don't give a fuck how much money we make, it will never change me. I'm always gon' be a killa."

"Nigga, you ain't changing because all of your money going up your nose or to the pharmacy. You still wanna jump down and kill shit because you are still a bum. The only mafuckas making any power moves is me and Smoke. You ain't contributing shit other than problems. Sand bag ass nigga." Tyson spat.

His words cut Greedy deep. "That's how you feel, nigga?"

"I don't speak unless I mean something." Tyson held the Mach Uzi more firmly on his lap. "You take that shit however you want to. I meant what I just said."

"Yeah, awright then, Tyson." Greedy snickered. "Bet those." He turned around and sat back in his seat. "We gon roll up in Pappy bowling alley where he and his killas be and see what's really good. How that sound, Smoke?"

Smoke nodded. "Cool, let's make it happen."

***

Smoke casually walked into Pappy's Bowlarama, with his Chanel black hoodie pulled all the way over his head and checked the time on his Patek. It was eleven o'clock on a hot night. When Smoke walked through the doors, the first thing he noticed was that the bowling alley appeared to be packed with a bunch of folks from the hood. There were ten females in tight shorts, skirts, and daisy dukes bowling in two groups of five. There were also nine dope boys bowling in just their shorts, and wife beaters. They had guns in their waistbands and had them displayed for all to see. Smoke was armed with two Glocks, and a bullet proof vest across his chest.

Smoke stepped into the bowling alley and surveyed the scene. He imagined each person inside of the establishment dead from multiple bullet holes inside of them. He felt giddy. If they would take four of his, then he wanted to take ten of theirs. It was about more than an eye for an eye for him. It was about supremacy, and the body count that went along with it.

"That nigga office right down that hallway. I don't see his punk ass out here, so he gotta be in there. I still don't know why you wanna talk to him first. You know his bitch ass ain't about to tell us shit."

"It's never about what a man says that tells you what you need to know, it's about what he does. It's important that I talk to him." Smoke looked down the hallway.

"Awright, well I'ma come back here with you to see what he's talking about." Greedy felt butterflies in his stomach.

Smoke headed in the direction of the hallway. He was about to stop at the counter when a short, dark skinned female came from around it with a pair of bowling shoes in her hand. Smoke pulled his hoodie forward so more as to shield his face. "Say, shawty, where is Pappy at?"

She pointed down the hallway. "He just went down the hall that way, toward this office, not two minutes ago. Do you have an appointment?"

"Why would I need an appointment to talk to my own cousin?" Greedy asked with his hoodie also pulled forward. "He just sent me a text, telling me to come straight back there when I get here. I'm from Arkansas."

"Oh, you from across that bridge on the other side then. See, I'm from Mississippi. But it's all good. Y'all come on." She led the way with both of them looking at her ass that was athletically built. When she got to the office, she knocked, and pushed on the door. It opened.

Pappy was sitting back in his seat getting his dick sucked by one of the hoes from West Memphis. "Whoa, whoa, whoa. Shawty, what I tell yo' crazy ass about knocking first?" He struggled to get his clothes in order. The girl stood back, wiping her mouth, and pulling down her short skirt.

"Dirty, you ain't tell me shit. I got a few potnas out hurr that say dey yo peoples. You need to see what's good with them." She moved out of the way.

Smoke entered the room first. He stood before Pappy's desk. "What's up, cuz?"

Greedy came inside. "Yeah, cuz, what's really good?"

The desk girl waved them off. "I gotta go get dis boy dese damn shoes." She closed the door behind her.

"Fuck is you niggas? Y'all ain't my mafuckin' peoples," Pappy snapped.

"Look, I'ma ask you this question one time. If you don't tell me the truth, I'm smoking you." Smoke pulled his hood back to reveal his face. In the death game, if a shooter revealed his identity, it was only because he wasn't expecting you to be alive when he left your presence. "Did you give the order for a few of yo lil' homies to come to the Mound and drop bodies?"

"What? Mane, y'all better get y'all goofy ass outta here wit' that shit. I mean it, do you know who the fuck I am?" Pappy asked.

Greedy upped his burner and pointed it at Pappy. He had a silencer on the end of it. The female hollered and dropped to the ground. "Bitch, shut up. Nigga, answer the question. Did you drop my lil' homies?"

"Mane, you pulled that banger out on me, now you better use it." Pappy stood up with a scowl on his face.

"No problem." Greedy aimed and pulled his trigger four quick times.

It was like Pappy saw the bullets coming at him in slow motion. They left out of Greedy's gun and zipped across the room toward his face. The first one burned into his cheek and knocked half of his face off. The second smacked a hole in his throat. The third punched through the middle of his neck, and the fourth blew through his forehead. He experienced the worst migraine that he ever had in all of his life, before he flew backwards, and his soul escaped his body. He ended up slumped on the floor with his eyes wide open. The girl began to scream at the top of her lungs.

Greedy came around the table and pumped four into her body, killing her instantly. Then he took off toward the front of the bowling alley. He aimed at the desk girl and popped her twice through the side of the head, killing her. She fell face first. He ran into the bowling area, pulling out his second gun, letting both of them ride, shooting every person in sight.

Smoke rushed the patrons and bucked down as many of the males as he could. He couldn't imagine a bunch of females shooting up the Mound, so he gave them a pass, but Greedy didn't. Greedy shot up everybody that he could see. He had no mercy. While his guns were still blazing, Smoke rushed into the security control room and took the entire DVD recording device that the security feed was going to.

By the time he came out of the back office, Greedy had finished off all of the patrons and was standing over them with his guns smoking. He didn't snap out of his zone until Smoke called his name and ran out of the bowling alley. Only then did Greedy curse, and then follow behind him. He looked back one time to see the bloody massacre that they had left behind, and then he was gone.

Chapter 11

It was a hot and humid Thursday morning, a couple days after the bowling alley massacre. The sun was shining in the cloudless blue sky, and the birds were flying about freely. Greedy rolled his Mercedes Benz G Wagon to the curb of Martin Luther King High School and beeped the horn as Eliza came out of the building with her Pink collection book bag draped over her right shoulder. She had been talking to two other friends. When she heard Greedy's horn, she looked up to see him nod at her.

Greedy rolled down the window and called out to her. Eliza froze, then she saw him waving for her to come over to the Wagon. She was confused, but slowly walked over to his Wagon while starting to text Tyson, her father.

Greedy placed a smile on his dark skinned face and looked her up and down. His eyes stopped on the swell of her breasts, and then something crossed his mind. What better way to get back at Tyson than to buss his oldest daughter down? He felt himself becoming hard.

Eliza stuck her head in the window. She was light skinned with light brown eyes, and a gorgeous face. Her hair was curly, and her body was curvy, so much so that she was rated the baddest female at her school. "Greedy, what are you doing here? I thought my dad was going to let me attend the pep rally tonight?"

"I don't know about all that, but I just came through to see if you wanna go shopping. I know that your birthday is coming up in a few weeks, and I wanted to be the first one to blow a bag on you. What's up?"

Eliza looked at Greedy from the side of her face. "You didn't talk to my dad about this, did you?" She watched him closely to see what his response was going to be.

Greedy thought about lying but worried how things would fair for him if she was to expose that he was. He knew that if she told Tyson that he had come to pick her up from school that he and Tyson were going to kill each other. Somebody was going to have to die, and as far as Greedy was concerned it was going to be Tyson. "You know I can't lie to that lil' pretty face. I ain't tell yo dad that I was coming because I know he would've shut it down because he thinks that you are still a baby, but I can see that you are a woman. I mean, look at you."

Eliza blushed. Tyson and her mother were so strict that they didn't allow for her to do anything, or to go anywhere. It had taken a bunch of begging before they relented to her going to a pep rally, and that was only because her friend Marsha was going along with her.

"Greedy, I would love to go, but my friend Marsha gotta go everywhere with me, or she's going to wind up telling on me. The reason why my mom and dad want me to stick by her is because they see her as a goodie two shoe, they know that she will report everything back to them. So thank you for the offer, but I just can't." Marsha called her name. She turned around to hear what she was saying.

When she turned around, Greedy's eyes went down to check out her ass. He saw how her jeans cuffed her backside, and how poked out she was. He shook his head. There was no way that he was about to pass up the opportunity to fuck Tyson's daughter. He was thirsty for her. "Say, Eliza, tell Marsha I'ma roll y'all to the game then. It's good, Uncle Greedy got you."

Eliza nodded, and jogged off to tell Marsha the new turn of events. When she got to her and explained the situation, she was shocked to find out that Marsha was planning on ditching the pep rally so that she could hang out for a few hours with her boyfriend, Xavier. They decided to meet back up at eight o'clock. Eliza was so happy that she jogged back to Greedy's Wagon and tried to open the door herself. He popped the locks and she pulled it open.

"What's good, Eliza? Where is your friend at?" The scent of her perfume wafted into the air and caused Greedy to feel some type of way.

"Don't worry about her. It turns out that all she wanted to do was spend some time with her boyfriend. You gon have to drop me back off at the school at seven forty-five. That way, me and her can link up at eight. Is that cool?"

Greedy's eyes were on her thick thighs. "Yeah, that's cool. I just wanted to spend some alone time with you anyway. You are so much older now." He pulled away from the curb.

"Well I couldn't stay a lil' girl forever, even though I know my daddy would've loved that." She pulled the seat belt across her chest and clicked it into place. "I still can't believe that you wanted to hit me up for my birthday, though. That's kind of cool."

Greedy laughed. "What, you don't think you're that important or something?"

She shrugged her shoulders. "I can never tell. My mama and daddy got so much stuff going on that it seems like they don't have time to really give me that attention that I need. Life is starting to get crazy, and now is the time when I feel like I need them the most, and they aren't here for me how I need them to be." She shook her head and exhaled loudly.

"Damn, lil' mama, I can only imagine what you're going through, but I'm here for you. If you need to talk about anything, my ears are open for you, and you can lean on my shoulder any day."

"Thank you, Uncle Greedy. That means a lot to me." She smiled, and then looked out of her passenger's window. "I wish my dad was like you sometimes. You seem so cool and so chill. He's always on me and sweating me about this or that. I can't do anything, and I am always in the house. That gets irritating after a while. I just wish that things were different."

Greedy was shaking. He felt the evil side of him fighting to take over his mind. He pulled a stuffed Kush blunt out of his ashtray and rolled up all of the windows in the Wagon. After sparking the blunt, he turned on some music.

"Eliza, I don't like you looking all sad and stuff. It's three o'clock right now, that means that you're about to be rolling with me for every bit of five hours. I want you to just sit back and chill. It's just me and you." He took another pull off of the blunt, and inhaled it deeply, before passing it over to her.

Eliza laughed and shook her head. "Unh, unh, my parents would kill me if they found out that I was high. I can't do that. I wish I could, but I can't."

"Baby girl, didn't I tell you that you were chilling with me for a few hours. Now this is how we're about to chill. Once we get up there, then we gon' blow this." He pulled ten thousand dollars out of a Gucci bag that was tucked in between the consoles. The money was in all forms of small bills, so it looked like it was way more than it actually was.

"You're about to spend all of that on me? Are you serious?" Eliza was so excited.

"And this is just today. Every time that me and you kick it from here on out, I'ma blow a bag on you, just so I can make sure that you always feel better when I leave you. You matter greatly to me. You're my lil baby. You know that. Now huh." He waved the blunt in her face again.

Eliza turned her head away from him. "But I still can't go home high. If they even sense that I am, I am going to be grounded for a long time."

"Look, we got five hours, right?"

"Right."

"Well, this Kush only lasts for three hours. We gon' go shopping during that time, and then I'll take you out to eat. And by the time I drop you off, you'll be sober as a pastor of a church. I got you, lil' baby. You should already know that. Now here. Just blow wit' me. Oh, and I'ma give you one of these, too. That way that bud will be gone out of your system for sure." He gave her two pink Mollies and handed her his spiked bottled water.

Eliza, full of peer pressure, popped the pills, and chased them with the water that Greedy had spiked with Mollie, and Percocets. She took the blunt from his hand and took three baby tokes of it. She inhaled them and began to choke like crazy.

"Drink the water, Eliza." He laughed, patting her back after rolling and stopping at a stop sign.

Eliza's throat felt raw. She downed the entire bottle of water and sat back trying to breathe. She closed her eyes. She could hear her heart pounding in her chest. "Dang, this stuff is harsh." She handed Greedy back the blunt and opened her eyes. Her head was spinning. The high slowly began to take over her until she was lifted.

Greedy took the blunt and pulled off from the stop sign. "I got you though, lil' baby."

Eliza sat back for a moment in silence. She closed her eyes again. "Dang, I'm starting to feel high already. Aw shoot." Her body began to tingle.

Greedy smiled and eyed her thighs again. She had them slightly parted. The jeans were all up in her little gap, forming a camel's toe print. *Her pussy fat*, he thought. "So where you wanna go, Eliza? We can go cop you some clothes from anywhere, or I can treat you like a true boss and just give you the cash for you to spend however you want to. Do you wanna do that?"

She opened her eyes. "That would be cool, because I can always order some stuff online later, and just pay my friends back whenever they use their credit cards to order it for me. I didn't know how I was going to explain all of the stuff you were going to buy me to my parents anyway. But if we are not going to go shopping, then what are we going to do?"

"I just wanna chill wit' you. You're so gorgeous and popular now. Unc just wanna be in your presence. We are about to roll out to my pad, that way I can count out this cash for you. Look at you, you're already a true boss because you got me working for you. Now ain't that something?"

Eliza snickered, the weed was getting stronger and stronger and the Mollie had yet to kick in. "You're funny, Greedy."

Greedy nodded and looked between her thighs again. She rubbed her gap and took her hand away. "Yeah, we gon' roll to my pad right now."

***

Eliza sat back on the couch and tilted her head toward the ceiling. She gasped. "Unn. Greedy, what are you doing? You gon get me in trouble."

Greedy rubbed the material between her thick thighs and pressed the panties into her lips. He had her jeans opened, with her thick thighs splayed. His hand was inside of the jeans and rubbing her fresh pussy through the material. She wore a pair of white panties with hearts all over them. Greedy found it crazy that Tyson and Ellie still dressed their daughter as if she were a real little girl, instead of a high schooler. Greedy sucked on her neck and slipped his hand into the pentode. He found her crease and played over the fat lips that were so wet it felt like she'd peed on herself. He kissed her neck. "They don't let you do nothing, do they, baby?"

The Mollie had Eliza's pussy on fire. She had never been so horny in all of her life. She humped his hand without even realizing that she was doing so. "No, Greedy, you know they don't."

Greedy dropped from the couch and pulled her panties down. Her light caramel pussy popped out at him. Her scent was heavy. He had her riled up, and it drove him crazy. He stuck his nose right on her gap, and sniffed hard, before he slurped her juices, and licked up and down her crease.

Eliza dug her nails into the cushions of the couch and moaned out loud. Her hard nipples were sticking through her bra like erasers. "Uh, Greedy, this is so wrong. You are not supposed to be doing this to me. Shoot."

Greedy peeled her lips apart to enjoy the view of her pinkness. Her little hole winked at him. He stuck his tongue into it and darted it in and out. He kissed her Pearl, and sucked on it, while his tongue went from side to side in a fast motion.

Eliza screamed, and bucked forward. She came hard for the first time in her life. "Uh. Uh. Uhhhhh, Greedy." Her kitty began squirting her delight back to back. It landed all over Greedy's cheeks, and nose. He kept eating until she pushed him away from her. She got up on wobbly knees, her juices leaked down her thighs. "I can't handle it. This is so wrong, Greedy. My daddy would go crazy.

Greedy stood up and pulled down his boxers. His dick was already at attention. He grabbed Eliza and bent her over the couch. He squeezed her juicy booty, before kicking her feet apart. He took his piece and rubbed it up and down her groove. He pushed forward into her heat. She was tight. His piece bent.

"Uhhh. Greedy, what are you doing?" She was leaking like crazy.

Greedy was determined. He held her waist steady and spread her pussy with his fingers. He cocked back and stabbed forward as hard as he could, burying half of his dick into her. She yelped, and then he gave her the rest. Then he was stroking her at full speed. *Bam. Bam. Bam. Bam.*

Eliza balled up her fist and beat on the couch because it felt so good. She couldn't believe that Greedy, her father's best friend, was fucking her. "Unnnnn." She screamed and began to drool at the mouth as he went into overdrive.

"Shit, lil' baby." *Bam. Bam. Bam. Bam.* "Uh fuck. You got that good pussy. You got that shit." He pounded harder and harder until he was cumming inside of her, stroking at full speed.

Eliza's eyes crossed. She whimpered, and came, feeling Greedy pound away at her. She knew what they were doing was wrong, but it felt so good. "Uhhh. Unc. Shoot."

Greedy turned her around and picked her up and kissed all over her lips. She shocked him when she kissed him back. He fell to the floor with her and slid back into her pussy. With no mercy he began to pound her out licking and sucking all over her neck. She clawed at his back and came hard. Greedy kept stroking. He ripped her bra open. Her breasts bounced up and down. He groaned looking at how pretty they were. He remembered when she didn't have anything. He groaned again.

"Eliza, I'm finna turn yo lil' ass out." He spent the next two hours trying to do just that.

Chapter 12

Phoenix knelt beside Natalia, and rubbed sun tan lotion into her belly, and then her arms and legs as the ocean water crashed into the sand in front of them. Seagulls screeched across the sunny skies. The heavy scent of the salt water from the ocean permeated through the air. The beach was packed already, even though it was only eight o'clock. Phoenix rubbed the lotion into Natalia's little toes. "Baby, can you tell me why you insisted on coming to the beach this early in the morning?"

Natalia straightened the big sun hat on her head and looked up to him from her Burberry shades. "I was feeling a little down, and the beach always makes me feel so much better. Why, do you not want to be here with me right now? You can go." She laid back and rested her right hand on her stomach.

Phoenix didn't feel like getting into an argument. For the last couple of days, Natalia had been acting very weird toward him, and he knew that it stemmed from him having not proposed to her like she wanted him to do. "Look, baby, I love you. You should know that you are my world. Why should we be beefing over this whole marriage thing when our relationship is fine the way that it is?"

"Phoenix, if you don't want to be here, you can leave. I need to clear my head, and this is where I am choosing to do it. If you have a problem with that, then bounce." She closed her eyes and smiled at the feel of the heat beaming off of her face.

"Say, shawty, you talking to me like I'm some kind of peon or somethin'. If yo ass wasn't pregnant, I'd fuck you up, Natalia. I don't give a fuck how many bodyguards you got."

She smirked. "Boy, bye. Ain't that what you Americans say?" She snickered.

Phoenix was red hot. Had Natalia been anybody else, or even been her and not pregnant, he would've done something to cause her pain. But while she held their child, she was precious, and there was no way that he could hurt her in any physical way. "You know what, Natalia? I'ma take a walk and blow off some steam. You better get yo mafuckin' attitude in check. I know you're feeling a lil' off because of this whole marriage thing, and you're about to give birth, so I'm going to be considerate and keep it pushing, with all of that in mind."

"Sounds like a good idea. Deuces." She held up two fingers.

"Yeah, whatever." He waved her off and walked away from her.

Natalia felt sick to her stomach. She hated being mean to Phoenix, but she felt so angry with him. *How could he be man enough to make her a mother, but not man enough to make her a wife?* She wondered. She sighed, and felt like crying, but she refused to allow for her emotions to overpower her. She sat up and glanced down the beach. She saw Phoenix seventy yards away talking with two Brazilian women that were as dark as him, and their hair was as long as hers. She grew jealous. Before she had time to fully dwell on it, a Russian woman sat next to her, and crossed her legs Indian style. Natalia didn't even look over at her. "So what did you find out?"

"According to prison records, your father was supposed to have been buried by the state of Tennessee, in Holy Land cemetery, three days after he was executed by the state."

"And did you have our people check this out to make sure that it was authentic?" Natalia asked, watching Phoenix with anger.

"They are on it right now, Natalia, but I can already tell you that somethin' is at bay here. The Warden of Bastrop has deep family ties to the Cartels all throughout Mexico. We've done our research, and I'm just telling you that somethin' is not adding up."

Natalia finally looked over to the petite ice blonde, she also wore sunglasses. "I am paying you a significant amount to find out just what is going on. There is no reason that you should be sitting here, if you do not have all of the facts. Are you understanding me, Porsava?" She spoke these words to her in Russian.

Porsava stood up. "Yes, ma'am. I will be in touch."

"Wait a minute. Help me up." Natalia reached up for her.

Porsava helped her to her feet. "Natalia, if it comes down that there is foul play going on, what do you want me to do?"

"Nothing. You come and tell me everything, and it is my job to react as I see fit to the news. Do you understand me?"

Porsava nodded. "I do. I will be in touch." She walked off with her long hair flowing behind her.

Natalia stood there for a moment, before she headed down the beach.

***

Phoenix laughed, and made the Brazilian girl do a spin so he could check out the rest of her body. She wore a G-string that sliced her melons in two. Her ass cheeks were dark brown and glistening. She was flawless, and he had to have her in one of his strip clubs. "Shawty, I know you don't speak that much English, but I'm about to buy a translator so we can communicate. I want yo lil' ass under contract like asap. Do you hear me?"

She understood every few words. She nodded and handed him her phone. "My number."

Natalia walked up, snatched the phone out of her hand, and threw the phone as far toward the water as she could get it. It landed by the sand and water line. She bumped Phoenix out of the way and faced the Brazilian.

"Bitch, he got a pregnant woman already. You need to take your roasted ass somewhere else so you can break up another couple's relationship."

"What?" The Brazilian asked.

"Bitch, go. Now." Natalia pointed at the water.

The Brazilian mugged her and balled up her fists. She looked down at Natalia's stomach and thought to give her a pass. She waved at Phoenix and walked away to retrieve her phone. Her ass jiggled the whole way.

Phoenix ran his hand over his deep waves. "I wanted to put her up in my new club that I'm opening up on the strip in three months. Why would you do that?"

"Because you think that I'm stupid. What type of man flirts, and tries to pick up a woman, while his pregnant girl-friend is literally in eye sight? Damn, you don't have no shame, do you?"

"Shawty, yo ass tripping. I would never do somethin' as reckless as that. I keep telling you that I love you more than what you give me credit for." He laughed.

Natalia smacked fire from him. Phoenix frowned and was about to punch her in her shit when her water broke. It spilled to the sand and created a mess. She fell against him.

"Aw shit, my water just broke, Phoenix. It's time."

"I know, and I got you. Come on."

***

Sabrina paced back and forward in the living room of her apartment with her mind filled with a thousand thoughts. Her brain was so full that she didn't know which thought to give more attention to first. She squeezed her fingers into a fist, and then shook them out. She looked over to Kevin as he sat in the kitchen eating the meal that she had prepared for him before he revealed to her that he was an actual FBI agent for the Department of Justice, and that he was investigating Phoenix, and the infamous Duffle Bag Cartel crew out of Memphis, Tennessee.

Kevin turned around, and stood up, wiping his mouth on a napkin. "Listen, I know you're thrown off, baby, but I promise you that this has nothing to do with you. We have been investigating Phoenix Stevens for over four years now, and according to our surveillance, informants, and a whole array of federal agents, he's in pretty deep. It's amazing the grand jury hasn't chosen to indict him just yet."

"Wait a minute, so you're thinking they are going to want to indict my cousin? Based on what charges?" Sabrina was worried. She didn't want to see Phoenix behind bars like a lot of their other family members. That was no life for a man to live. She was sure that she would support him no matter what, but she still didn't want to see him go through that.

"Right now, the investigation is ongoing, and I am not supposed to divulge any information regarding the case. What I will say to you is this, though, any money that Phoenix Mitchell-Stevens has given you over the years, it makes you guilty of aiding and abetting, and also conspiracy. The authorities are going to want to talk with you soon, and they may be asking you to give up any information of crimes that you know he has committed. If you withhold any information, you can potentially be targeted for a crime. The only reason I am telling you this is because I genuinely care for you, despite my job." He came to her to take a hold of her arms.

Sabrina jerked away from him. "You lying son-of-a-bitch. You don't care about me. All of it was a ruse to get close to my cousin. You were on to us when we first came to Miami over six months ago. You used me and got what you wanted. You're a sick man."

"Sabrina, I honestly fell for you. You are an amazing woman, and if I were not already happily married, I would have pursued you to make you my wife right away. You are perfect for me."

"We fucked, Kevin. If you were so happily married, how could you lay down with me, and sleep with me? That makes no sense. You're a dog, and that's all you ever will be. I hate your guts, and I'm not going to let you bitches take my cousin away from me."

"Your cousin or your man? Which is he?" He stepped forward. "I mean, because I have audio and visual footage that says he could fall under any umbrella. So which is he?"

"More of a man than you will ever be. And whatever we want to do, we do, and we don't give a fuck about what this world thinks. So keep your comments, and your thoughts to yourself because they don't matter. All we care about is us." She walked to the front of the door and opened it. "Leave my house, Kevin."

"Sabrina, if I didn't care about you, I would have never revealed to you who I really am. The fact that I'm telling you what it is should let you know that I care about you. That has to count for something."

"I found your badge and looked up the number on my fuckin' own. You weren't going to tell me shit. Don't act like you're doing me a favor, because you're not. You don't care about me, but my cousin, Phoenix, does."

Kevin shook his head. "You need to prepare for Phoenix to be removed from the picture. His clock is ticking. If you care about Shante, you will take custody of her when he is removed. Toya wants nothing else to do with neither her nor

Phoenix. She's a cooperating witness. And once again, I've said way too much."

Toya snitching? That bitch, Sabrina thought. "Kevin, or should I say Agent Jones, can you please leave my home?"

Kevin walked up to her and smiled in her face. "I really do wish you the best. You are a really nice person. But your sickness for Phoenix will be the death of you. Mark those words. Create you some distance. It's imperative that you do so." He stepped into the hallway, and looked her up and down, remembering their last passionate night. "Sabrina, I will always lo..."

Slam.

Sabrina slammed the door in his face and locked it. "Fuck. I gotta get to the hospital so I can let Phoenix know what is going on," she said out loud, while grabbing her Lexus keys. One of the two Lexus's that Phoenix had bought for her. She couldn't believe that there was a chance that he could be taken away from her. She grabbed her purse and threw open the door. She ran smack dead into a six feet four inch, Italian Federal Agent with a scowl on his face.

"Mrs. Stevens, I am Federal Agent Tony Busca, and this is Federal Agent Rawlings." He nodded at his Black female partner. "We need to ask you a couple questions."

"I don't have anything to say to y'all. Move, please."

Tony Busca slid into her way. "Ma'am, we're going to do this here, or at the station. Either way it's happening." His partner slid beside him.

Sabrina looked over them both, and sighed. "Shit, man, what do y'all wanna know?"

Ghost

Chapter 13

Phoenix held his son in his arms, then removed him from his chest so he could look over his yellow face. It looked a little reddish to him, but nevertheless, he felt like he was the most beautiful baby boy that he had seen in all of his life. He felt weak for him. He kissed the baby's forehead and placed him back securely to his chest again. "Man, I love you already."

Natalia scooted upward in the bed. "You're supposed to, he's your son. Oh, and guess what? He has ten fingers and ten toes. He's not an alien. Arrgh." She made scary hands and waved them all around as if she were a monster.

"Ha, ha, ha." He eyed her and smirked his face. "He is the cutest baby boy that I have ever seen, though. How are you feeling?"

"Weak. I don't have any energy right now. I wanna kick yo' tail for allowing me to have this child without first becoming a wife, but it's all good. I know who I'm dealing with." She fluffed her pillows and laid her head back on it.

Phoenix brought the baby over and sat on the edge of her hospital bed. He kissed her on the forehead. "Thank you for giving me such a beautiful baby. I can never repay you for this gift. It means the world to me." He kissed her forehead again.

"I still find it ironic that you are able to get everything that you want and need, but when it comes to me, I am only able to get what you think I deserve. That is so unfair." She crossed her arms in front of her chest.

"Baby, the only thing you've asked me for that I haven't given you is the whole marrying thing. I will give you anything else, I just think that getting married is overdoing it. I will give you absolutely anything else, other than that. Just name it."

"Phoenix, nothing else matters more than that. God, don't you get it? Even though our relationship is taboo, we have already ran the entire gambit. Why wouldn't you become my husband? In my culture, if a woman has a child out of wedlock, and does not marry the father, she is an outcast. She is considered despicable, and the child is considered cursed. I do not wish for our child to be cursed. Everything can't always be about you and what you feel, either. Sometimes you have to consider other people's feelings and standpoints."

"Well, give me some time to think about that, but for now, I need to know what we are going to name our son? And just being on some player shit, I'ma let you name him whatever you wanna name him."

"Watch your mouth around our child, and I already know what I am going to name him. He will be called Phoenix Taurus Stevens."

The baby kicked its legs and laughed while it slept. Phoenix's eyes lit up. Natalia smiled. Phoenix kissed him on the forehead.

"You sure that's what you want his name to be?" He asked, stroking her cheek.

"I am sure, and that's what it will be." She removed his hand from her cheek and reached for their son.

Phoenix handed him over to her. "What about us? Do you think that we will ever be able to be happy with one another again, now that we have a child together?"

"Why would us having a child together ruin our relationship? If anything, it should strengthen it." She held their son closer to her, and then pulled back her gown and began fitting her nipple into his mouth. He latched on hungrily.

"I'm just saying, you already know how it goes after a child is born. Everything becomes all about it, and no longer about the parents. That's how a lot of couples fall off. I just wanna make sure that we don't."

Natalia closed her eyes for a moment. The whole breasts feeding thing was still obviously new to her and she had to get used to it. "Phoenix, you're just self-centered, and you're used to everything revolving around you. Now that we have a baby, you're going to have to share some of the spotlight, and that terrifies you."

Phoenix stood up and mugged her. "You think you know me so well Natalia, but you don't. What I'm feeling ain't got nothin' to do with my son. The reason I am asking you these questions is because you were still talking about this marriage shit and I ain't feeling it."

Natalia scoffed. "I love you, Phoenix, but right now, I hate your freaking guts, too. What I need is for you to get out of my face for a few minutes. You're irritating me, and it's driving me crazy. Bye, boy." She began to mumble in Russian.

Alicia knocked on the door, and poked her head in. "Knock, knock, y'all, I came to see the baby and to say congratulations." She came all the way into the room. Her eyes immediately saw that the baby looked healthy and strong as it sucked on Natalia's big, brown nipples.

"Well here he is." Natalia scooted closer to the side of the bed.

Alicia looked him over and saw that he was handsome. The baby opened his eyes to reveal that he had grayish blue eyes. This made Alicia mad, for some reason that she couldn't understand. She had a vision of stabbing Natalia in the back with a butcher's knife. "Wow, he is really cute, and he already has a head full of curly hair." *Mixed bitch*, she thought. "So, what did y'all name him?"

"His name is Phoenix Taurus Stevens." Natalia was proud of his name. She wanted to slap Alicia in the face with the knowledge of it all. She could see the jealousy written all over her mug. It delighted her.

"Y'all named him Phoenix, for real?" She felt her stomach drop. She looked over to Phoenix. He had his back to them. "Wow, well that's cool, I guess. I wish y'all the best." She stormed out of the room.

"Drive safely," Natalia called.

Phoenix mugged her. "You're petty as hell, and you know it." He shook his head and left behind Alicia.

***

He didn't catch up with her until she was getting into her Lexus truck. She slammed the door when he called her name. She started the engine.

Phoenix appeared at her passenger's door, pulling on the handle of it. "Alicia, let me in."

Alicia revved the engine. She mugged him. "You didn't give a fuck about our son, Phoenix. You just didn't."

"Man, open the mafuckin' door before I bust this window out," he snapped.

"Why, Phoenix? Why would you do some bullshit like that?" she screamed.

"Alicia, on my word, if you don't open this mafuckin' doe, I'ma bust this bitch ass window out. Pop that mafuckin' lock. Right now."

Alicia popped the locks, and he slid into the truck. "Ma, that name shit ain't have nothing to do wit' me. She hollering this marriage thing, and I ain't ready for that. So to appease her, I told her that she could name our child whatever she wanted, and these are the names that she came up with."

"That bitch hates my guts. She did this shit to spite me. But how can a woman be so petty? My son was killed. He was your firstborn, and he was supposed to carry your name until he buried us. Why is she trying to steal his birthright? He was innocent, Phoenix." She covered her face and began to cry her eyes out.

Phoenix felt lower than a sewer. He rubbed her back. "Alicia, I'm sorry. I swear, I didn't have nothing to do with the process."

She raised her head from her hands and mugged him. "As long as I knew you, I've never known for you to be soft, or for you to act like a bitch ass nigga. But now that is what you have turned into, a straight bitch nigga. If I was a man, I would beat yo ass, and make that killa shit come back out of you, because right now, I can't see it. Where the fuck is it? What, since that bitch yo cousin and you fucking, you feel like you gotta play pussy or somethin'?" She scrunched up her face, and mugged him, the mama bear coming out of her.

"You betta watch yo mafuckin' mouth, shawty. Who do you think you're talking to?"

"I'm talking to the bitch version of you, nigga. Now what?"

Phoenix felt his temper rising. "Say, Alicia, I know you're going through some thangs right now, and what Natalia just did is pissing you off, but baby you can't take that shit out on me. I am not the enemy."

"Yes, you are, Phoenix. Since day one, you've been the enemy. If I had never gone behind Mikey's back, screwing around with you, I wouldn't be in such turmoil right now. You have always been my weakness. Ever since you came into my life, I have never been able to resist you." Tears came down her cheeks. "She crushed me with that decision to name y'all baby after mine. Phoenix, that was our son's name. I'm gonna get that bitch back. I swear to God, I am." She cried harder.

She covered her face again, and went into a fit of heavy breathing, and groaning.

"Damn, Alicia, please don't do this shit to me. You already know I can't take you breaking down like this."

"You wouldn't let her do this, Phoenix, if I was related to you. If you and I had the same blood, you would protect and love me how you love her and Sabrina, or Kamya, for that matter. But since I am not a part of y'all bloodline, you allow me to be shitted on. You ain't said one word about avenging our baby's death. Them niggas back there in Memphis living their lives like kings, all on our son's blood, and you ain't did shit." She reached out and punched him in the mouth, and then the eye. Then she was screaming and scratching at him like a maniac, remembering how Phoenix Jr. looked in a casket. She cried harder.

Phoenix pushed her back and held her hands. "Alicia, Alicia, baby, I'm sorry. I'm sorry. I love you, and my son. I didn't even think that far into things."

Alicia yanked her hands away from him. "That's the fuckin' problem right there. Had it been one of them, or a baby that you had by one of them, you would have blown Memphis off of the map, with no hesitation. You don't give a fuck about me, but it's good, though." She started the truck and pulled out of the space.

Phoenix sat there feeling like a got damn fool because Alicia was right. He wondered why he hadn't felt the need to go back to Memphis to avenge his son's death. Had it been anybody that was a part of his family, he would've never left until the job was done. So why did he leave Memphis and never give the revenge a second thought? The question plagued him. "Alicia, you're right."

"I don't wanna hear it, Phoenix."

"N'all, on some real shit, you really are right. I gotta do something about our baby. As his father, and out of the unconditional love that I have for you, I gotta go back and make them niggas feel my pain at all costs. It ain't no other way around it. You're right about me acting like a bitch, too. I feel like I've been losing myself ever since I left Tennessee, but I'm about to bounce back and make some heads roll. Fuck all this weak shit, it's time for me to get back to the old me."

Alicia nodded. "I wanna see Smoke's head on a platter. I'm not playing, either, Phoenix. I wanna see his head on a platter, and I want Mikey's actual heart. If you bring me these two things then I will be able to start the process of healing over the real Phoenix Jr. But until then, I am forced to walk around with my heart broken. It's not fair, and it ain't cool. You owe me blood. I want blood, Phoenix." She began to shake and looked over at him.

Phoenix nodded his head in agreement. "That I do, and that's what you are going to get. I'm going back to Memphis, and these fuck niggas about to feel my pain."

Chapter 14

It was eleven at night, on a cool Tuesday night. Greedy pulled into the dark alley behind Tyson's home, and scooted down as low as he could inside of the truck. A minute after he parked, he texted Eliza that he was there. Eliza climbed out of her bedroom window and fell to the grass. She ran across the backyard until she made it to the alley. Once there, she jogged to Greedy's truck and slipped into the passenger's seat. He slowly eased down the alley.

Eliza came across the console and kissed him on the lips. "Greedy, I missed you. I've been thinking about you every second of every day. It's driving me crazy." She reached into his lap and squeezed his dick. She groaned. "Are we going to your house, baby?"

Greedy nodded. "You sho' you can wait that long, though?"

She groaned again. "I don't know, I hope so." She licked his neck and sucked on his ear lobe.

Greedy grabbed her ass. She had on a short skirt that he'd bought for her. It barely covered her backside. He'd told her to not wear panties. He slid his hand under it to make sure that she didn't. When he discovered that her pussy was naked as the day she was born into the world, he became hard. "Baby, sit in yo' seat for a minute."

She followed his commands. Her kitty was already oozing and thirsty for him. "I missed you, Unc. Did you miss me?"

Greedy laughed. "You're my lil' baby, of course I missed you."

"I think I need you worse than ever, Greedy. I don't know what you've done to me, but you drive me crazy." She ran her fingers between her lips and slipped her middle finger into herself. She pulled it out and sucked all over it.

Greedy waited until he stopped at a red light. He pulled a Mollie out of his pocket and slipped it into Eliza's pussy as deep as he could. She moaned and brought her feet on to her little toes. She arched her back with her mouth wide open. Greedy took a second one and pushed it equally deep. "This pussy ready for daddy, ain't it?" It was oozing.

She nodded. "I want you so bad. It's driving me crazy." She squeezed her young breasts and sucked her bottom lip.

Greedy pulled off at the light and kept rolling. "You sho' they ain't gon be asking no questions about where you are?"

"My mama and daddy are having their date night tonight. I told my mother that I have cramps and told my father that it was that time of the month. He never messes with me when he thinks that I am on my cycle. It's a sure way to keep him at bay."

"You did good then, baby. Daddy gonna take good care of you tonight then. Do you trust me?" He rubbed all over her left thick thigh and pulled it apart so he could see her sex lips. They were juicy, and slightly wrinkled with dew on them.

"Yes, I trust you," she moaned.

Then open yourself for me. Let me see that lil' hole that drives me crazy." He turned on the interior lights.

Eliza arched her back again and opened her little lips. She made sure that he could see her little hole that looked like it was pea sized. "You see it, daddy?"

"Hell yeah, I do. Aiight, that's all I needed to see." He cut the lights and pulled away from the curb.

***

Tyson held Ayesha close to his chest as they danced slowly to the Mary J Blige track coming out of the speakers. He kissed her neck. They had been together for seventeen years, and through it all, she had always been one hunnit to him. Ayesha was the only person in the world that Tyson knew he could be with for the rest of his life.

Ayesha looked up to her husband and kissed his neck. "Thank you for bringing me out tonight, baby. It really means a lot."

"Stop playin, we are supposed to make sure that we have a date night every week. It's important so that our relationship will flourish." He turned her around and dipped her.

"I still wanted to give you your props for making the effort, though. You could be one of those dope boys that roam the streets always looking for somethin' new, but you're not. You're right here with me, and I love you so much for it." She hugged him tighter, and slowly grooved to the music.

"The only reason I'm in the streets is so I can take care of our family. A man ain't a man if he doesn't provide for his family. Baby, now that I got these Bread Gang rappers, it opened up a whole new market of money for our family. We don't gotta sell dope no more. All of our shit can be legit now. It's time that I start to make a legacy for our children, and for us. I'm tired of being in the streets, and I am tired of putting our family under the gun. Y'all deserve better than what I've been providing, and that's just the honest to God truth." He had a quick flash of all of the negative things that he'd done that put his family under the gun, and he shook his head. "I'm ready to step away from the game, Ayesha, and that's just how I feel."

"Honey, I am your wife, and I will support you in whatever you do that is positive. You already know that I got your back. You are the head of this family, and you are the love of my life. I promise I'ma hold you up. That's my job."

Tyson felt like a billion bucks. "I got enough cash put up to pay for Eliza's college now. That was my goal after I bought you a house. Now my goal is to fully acclimate myself into this music industry and take the world by storm. After that, the sky's the limit for you and my lil' girl."

"Well, like I said, I will support you with all that I am. That's my job." She kissed his neck. "Come on, baby, let's get out of here." She took his hand and pulled him toward the exit of the lounge.

Tyson laughed, "Aw, you must be ready for me to tap that ass back there?"

"Boy, hush, you ain't gotta let everybody know what I like done to my derrière. Dang." She switched her hips and looked back at him. "But I am ready, though." She laughed.

They made it into the parking lot, and to the Lincoln Navigator. Tyson chirped the alarm and popped the locks on the door. Then a masked Phoenix and two of his hittas came from between the cars that were parked on the side of them. Phoenix pointed his gun directly at Ayesha. "Bitch, don't move or I'ma blow yo shit so far back they gon think you're a drop top."

Ayesha put her hands up in the air. "Please, don't shoot."

Tyson thought about the Glock .40 that was under his driver's seat. "What is this, a robbery? If it is, I got a few thousand in the truck. You can have it just let me and my wife go. We got a daughter."

Phoenix walked up to Ayesha and slammed the handle of his gun into her forehead as hard as he could. She dropped to the ground. "Bitch nigga, don't move, you and I have some unfinished bidness to attend to."

***

Greedy placed Eliza's right ankle up on his shoulder, and then added her left. He slid back into her pussy and began long stroking her with reckless abandon. Her pussy got wetter and wetter with each thrust inside of it. Greedy grunted and growled as he dug her out. "Tell me who daddy is? Tell me?"

Eliza squeezed her eyes tighter. "You my daddy. Aw shoot, Greedy, you my daddy."

"Huh. Huh. Huh. Daddy loves his baby. You my lil' baby." He dug deeper, her walls wrapped around his piece, and sucked him further into her body. He licked on her slender ankle and kept thrusting.

The headboard knocked against the wall. The bed squeaked loudly. Half of the covers were on the floor. Eliza dug her nails into his waist and pulled, scratching him. The Mollie inside of her womb was driving her crazy. It heightened all of her senses and made her crave Greedy. She was becoming sexually obsessed with him. She pulled him down so she could lick all over his lips.

"Okay, okay, what about me?" Marsha asked. She was riled up from watching them, and now she wanted in. Eliza had convinced her, after Greedy's constant urging, to join them for a night of chilling, after they picked her up, Greedy handed her a blunt, and Eliza gave her a bottled water that was spiked with four pink Mollies of nearly pure MDMA. She was oozing between the thighs and going insane. She dropped her skirt and crawled on the bed. She kissed all over Greedy's back and rubbed between their sexing bodies until she could feel Greedy driving in and out of Eliza.

Eliza screamed and came. She sucked Greedy's lips hungrily. "I love you, daddy. You're my daddy. You're mine." She came again and tried to push him off of her.

Greedy pounded her out and felt himself cumming. He pulled out and held her sex lips open while he came on her pink pearl. Her little gap was wide open because of him. He snickered and came over and over until she was filled with his cream. Then he fell backward on the bed.

Marsha took a hold of his piece and held it in her hand. She pumped it in her white fist. Greedy's black, grown piece had been the first she had ever seen in real life. It fascinated her. She squeezed it tightly and brought a drop of cum to the top of it before she licked it off. "Mmm." She sucked the head into her mouth and went to town.

Greedy slid his hand between her pink thighs and rubbed her naked box. She shivered. He dipped a finger into her hole and found it tight. "Damn, lil' shawty, I thought white girls be getting it in?" He sucked his fingers and slid it back into her.

"My parents are too strict. I'm a virgin like she was." Marsha closed her eyes while Greedy manipulated her clitoris.

Eliza kissed all over Greedy's chest. "Daddy, you don't love her more than me, do you?" She bumped Marsha out of the way and took hold of Greedy's dick.

Marsha pushed her and grabbed it back. "No, it's my turn." She tried to put Greedy into her mouth.

Eliza took it out and sucked it into hers. "Mine, tell her, daddy."

Greedy grew back to full mast. He slapped Eliza's hand off of him and grabbed Marsha so fast that her blonde hair went all over her face. He straddled her and opened her thighs. "You want some of this Orange Mound shit, shawty, huh? Think this lil' pussy can handle it?" He separated the folds with the head of his dick.

Marsha closed her eyes as she felt him boring into her. He stuffed her, and pulled out, then he slammed it back home again. "Unh. Unh. Unh. Shit. You big mutha..." She opened her thighs wider and summoned him to fuck her harder. "Do it. Do it. Please, do it."

Greedy ripped open her blouse and displayed her pale titties with the cherry colored nipples. He cocked back and slammed forward as hard as he could. She screeched and locked her ankles around him. "Yeah, don't get scared now. It's on." He growled. He got to fucking her at full speed for ten minutes straight. They fell on their sides. He pulled her hair and continued to pound into her ass. His dick dug deeper and deeper.

"Uh. Uh. Eliza, you made him fuck me like this. Shit." She squeezed tears out of her eyes and came. "Uh, this big black... Shit." She came again. "From behind. From behind. Please fuck me from behind like the movies."

Greedy flipped her over and pulled her to all fours. He slid back into her gap that sucked him back into her body. He held her narrow hips and zoned out, watching this black piece tear into her pink pussy until he came in her twice. Then he pushed her off of him and laid beside her still rubbing her naked slit. "Eliza, make this bitch eat yo lil' coochie, baby girl."

"What?" Eliza walked over to him on her knees. She'd been watching them and going to town on herself.

"You heard me. I wanna see it. Come here."

Eliza came over to him. "Yes, daddy?"

Greedy pulled her to him and kissed her lips. "You love me right?" He sucked her neck.

"Yes, I love the hell out of you." She moaned as he began to rub her pussy again.

"Then I wanna see this lil' white girl eat yo kitty, baby. What, are you scared or something?"

"No, I ain't scared. I'll do whatever you tell me to do." She kissed him again.

"Lay back, then, and let her do her thing."

Seconds later, Eliza laid back while Marsha crawled between her thighs and began to eat her like a lesbian. Eliza screamed, and hollered. She came and begged Greedy to fuck her. Greedy slipped behind Marsha and began to pound her out again, while she ate Eliza. He went faster, and faster the he went, the more of a show they put on for him, until he was cumming in Marsha again.

Eliza grew jealous. She pushed Marsha off of Greedy and hopped on top of him. She reached back and slid him into her gap and rode him at full speed. "You're mine. You're mine. Shoot, I love you so much." She laid stomach to stomach, popping on him until she came again, and passed out from exhaustion.

Chapter 15

Phoenix took the hammer out of his tool box and snickered to himself. He rubbed over the metal portion of it before he held the long wooden handle in his right hand. He pulled off his mask. Tyson gasped. Phoenix looked down at Tyson. Tyson had both of his wrists duct taped to the chair, along with his ankles, as well. Phoenix neglected to have his mouth taped, he wanted to hear what the man had to say. He had a series of questions he wanted to ask him, and Tyson's responses were very important.

Phoenix walked past Ayesha and rubbed her soft cheek. "After all of these years, yo lil' ass is still a pure dime. I should've taken you down more than once, back in the day." He pulled her low cut dress back and revealed her braless breasts.

"Hey, come on, Phoenix, man. This shit ain't got nothing to do with Ayesha. This is between me and you. Let my lady go so she can take care of my daughter. I would do that for you." Tyson pleaded, a line of sweat poured down the side of his face. He was shaking in his chair as he watched the big masked body guards that stood behind Phoenix slide their hands into leather gloves.

"Oh, would you now? Ain't you the same mafucka that stood back and watched Smoke kill my son? Or was it Mikey? Which one was it?" Phoenix asked, feeling his temper rising.

"Say, mane, I wouldn't never hurt no lil' shawty. I don't get down wit' that snitching shit, but all I can tell you is that I would have never supported them doing anythang to dat baby. They do they own thang, Phoenix, you already know how dis shit go." Tyson grew nervous when a small wooden table was slid next to him, and two of Phoenix's henchmen took his right hand and cuffed the wrist to a metal hook connected to the table. Then they held his hand flat out.

"N'all, mane, y'all ain't gotta hold his shit. Go stand right next to Ayesha. If this mafucka doesn't follow and do what I say, rip one article of clothing off of her at a time. I have known this fool for a long time, he loves this bitch. She is his weakness."

"Phoenix, you and I have always been respectful toward one another. Please don't do me like this," Ayesha begged.

Phoenix stepped in front of her and slapped her as hard as he could, splitting her lip. Ayesha spit blood across the room. Phoenix took a hold of her hair. He leaned into her face, while Tyson tried to break his binds, and kissed her cheek. Then he kissed her lips. "Bitch, you already know how I get down. I'm the reason you quit fuckin' wit cold blooded killas and settled for this sometime ass murderer right there. All this whining, and crying don't do shit for me. When I leave this basement tonight, I'm going to have everything I want, and you better pray that you still have your life." He muffed her and walked over to a seething Tyson. "Fuck you looking so stupid fo?"

"What you wanna know, Phoenix? What do you wanna know?" Tyson hollered.

"Which one of you lil' niggas killed my son?" Phoenix leaned into his face.

"Phoenix, the only thing I'm cool with telling you is what I did. I sweated a few of your original Duffle Bag Cartel niggas but I would never hurt a child. That ain't in me to do so. That's all I can tell you."

Phoenix brought the hammer down at full speed and crashed it into Tyson's pinky finger smashing it so hard that it exploded. Blood shot across the wooden table, and a bone poked out of his skin.

It took Tyson a second to understand what had happened. He looked down at his finger and back up to Phoenix before he opened his mouth and hollered as loud as he could in pain and agony.

Phoenix punched him square in the mouth. "Shut yo ass up."

Tyson's head ricocheted on his neck. His two front teeth loosened. His head fell forward in his lap. Blood dripped from his lips. He slowly looked over to Ayesha. She was whimpering over the state of his injury, and where she thought things were about to go.

"I ain't got no time to be playin' wit' you, Tyson. Somebody killed a baby. I ain't taking that shit lightly. You gon' tell me who did or shit about to get real bloody. It's as simple as that." He peeped Tyson's bloodied pinkie finger. He brought the hammer up and then down again on his entire right hand, shattering the bones within it.

Tyson hollered out in pain again, but then caught himself. He bit into his bottom lip, and sniffled. He looked over to Ayesha. "Man, Phoenix, you know the code in the Duffle Bag Cartel, we don't do that snitching shit. It seems to me like you're trying to make me break that code. You put it in place, potna."

Bam. Bam. Bam. Bam.

The hammer slammed into his hand over and over. It broke a series of bones with each contact. Phoenix raised it and brought it down again and again. He flipped it around to the extractors and pinned them into Tyson's hand.

"Smoke. Muthafucka. Smoke killed yo shawty, but Mikey told him to do it." Tears ran down his eyes. The wooden table was filled with his blood. It dripped off of the table onto the floor.

Phoenix knelt down in front of him. He slapped his hand on his shoulder. "Where were you when all of this was taking place?"

Tyson squeezed his eyelids together. "Why, Phoenix? What difference does that make?"

Phoenix snickered. "I'm going to ask you one more time. Where were you when all of this was..."

"I was right there, muthafucka. Got damn. I was right there, but what do you want me to do? Mikey is a fuckin' loose cannon, and so is Smoke. What did you want me to tell them to do, stop? I don't control them, Phoenix. I didn't touch your son, though, and I didn't touch Alicia."

Phoenix stood up and walked over to Ayesha. He knelt beside her and placed his hand on her left thigh. Ayesha was strapped. He squeezed her thigh. "Where is Eliza?"

Tyson felt like he was going to be sick. "What?"

"You heard me, nigga. I wanna know where that thick ass daughter of yours is? I just wanna talk to her." Phoenix snickered.

"Man, she's just a baby, Phoenix. What the fuck is you saying?" Tyson spit blood on the side of his chair.

"How old is she now, sixteen?" Phoenix shook his head. "Last time I saw her, she was popping out of those jeans. I still can't believe she grew all of that ass in one summer. I know she gives them boys at school hell. She gets it from her mama, though." He looked up to Ayesha. "Ain't that right, shawty?"

Ayesha felt her face still stinging from when Phoenix slapped the taste out of her mouth. "Please, don't say that, Phoenix. She is all that we have, and you're her Godfather."

"At one point in time, my son was all that me and Alicia had together. What makes Eliza lil' fine ass so different? Does he know?" Phoenix glanced over to Tyson.

Ayesha acted like she didn't hear the question. She closed her eyes and started to cry. She was shaking so bad that the chair was rattling on the floor. She swallowed her spit and took a deep breath.

"He doesn't, do he? Aw, this shit is fuckin' amazing. You mean to tell me that this nigga don't know that Eliza is really Mikey's daughter?" Phoenix started busting up laughing.

Tyson felt like his heart just stopped working. For a few moments he couldn't breathe. He closed his eyes. "What is he talking about, Ayesha?"

Ayesha whimpered. "I don't know, baby. You already know how Phoenix is."

"How am I? You dumb ass nigga. You been fucking with shawty for all of these years, and it didn't dawn on you that y'all only had one child, as much as you probably been bussing in her ass. What, you thought she was taking birth control pills or somethin'?" He shook his head at Tyson's ignorance.

Ayesha began to shake harder. "Please don't do this, Phoenix. Please don't ruin my family."

"So then it's true. Eliza is Mikey's daughter? You fucked that trifling ass nigga?" Tyson asked in disbelief.

Ayesha lowered her head. "I was young and dumb. I had a fascination with dope boys and Glock toters."

"Is she my daughter? Tell me. Please."

"I don't know, Tyson, but you are the only father that she knows, no matter what. Phoenix why are you doing this?" Ayesha whimpered.

"Cause the shit is hilarious. Ayesha is the mafuckin' reason I could never take a bitch seriously. You hoes be plotting and scheming just like us niggas do. Now one of you mafuckas finna tell me where Eliza is? I know she has gotten way more strapped since the last time I saw her, and I'm finna see what that be like."

"She is only fifteen. She's a kid, Phoenix." Ayesha couldn't look over to Tyson anymore. She felt embarrassed and ashamed.

"All of these years, I've been taking care of that lil' girl and fighting to give her the best possible life that she could have, and it turns out that she might be Mikey's baby? All along, this nigga was fuckin' you behind my back? What type of shit is that Ayesha? Huh?" He tried to break out of his binds.

Ayesha was in tears now. "I haven't slept with anybody other than you for almost sixteen years. Sixteen."

"That's probably why you ain't been pregnant in that long." Phoenix laughed.

"Fuck you." Tyson snapped. "Fuck you, Phoenix. Fuck you and Mikey. Y'all got everybody in the cross fires of this punk ass war that the two of you are waging against each other when it doesn't have anything to do wit' nobody other than you two mafuckas. This is bullshit and you know it. Mikey and Smoke killed yo shawty, we ain't have nothin' to do wit' it."

"That's your story?" Phoenix asked walking up on him with a hammer dripping blood.

Tyson mugged him. "Nigga, what do you want from me, huh? You got me in a basement. You smashed up my fingers and broke my hand. You bust me in my shit, so yeah, what do you want from me?"

Phoenix pressed his lips against Ayesha's cheek. "I wanna know where Mikey and Smoke is. You tell me that and you might get to live to see another day." He slid his hand up Ayesha skirt and found her naked between her thighs. He searched until she found her opening and went inside of her with two digits. "You ain't fucked nobody but this nigga right here for over fifteen years? Damn, this pussy gotta be the bomb by now because I remember you telling me how small this fool was. Remember that?" He dug his fingers deep into her pussy.

Ayesha shuddered, and moaned uncontrollably. She closed her eyes. "Stop talking, Phoenix. You're ruining my marriage."

Phoenix ran his fingers in and out of her. "Where are they, Tyson, or are you going to keep that secret as well, in the name of the Duffle Bag Cartel?" Phoenix pulled his fingers out and looked at them. They were sticky, with Ayesha's secretions on them. He slid them back into her box and sped up the pace.

Ayesha hopped in the chair. She tilted her head back and whimpered. "Please. Phoenix."

"Yeah, I can tell this shit ain't been hit right." He really got to digging all in her.

"Mikey stayed over in Evanston. Smoke stayed in Dalton. I'll give you their addresses and even take you to their spots. That nigga Mikey got that Coronavirus, though. They had him quarantined for a minute. Smoke fuck wit' me the long way. I can get him to come out, and you can handle yo' bidness with him. Just let me and my wife go, Phoenix. You're ruining us."

Phoenix was too busy circling his thumb around Ayesha's clitoris. He fingered her at full speed without ceasing. She shuddered and shivered. Her pussy was getting wetter and wetter. He sucked on her right inner thigh. "You finna cum, bitch. I know these shakes. I'm finna make yo bitch cum right in front of you, Tyson." Phoenix stuck his head between her thighs and blew on her clit, while he manipulated it. His tongue flicked across her nub for old time sake.

Ayesha bucked. She bit into her bottom lip. She tried to break her binds, and then got so embarrassed when she came, screaming at the top of her lungs. She began to shake uncontrollably in the chair, jerking into Phoenix's face.

Tyson felt like he'd been hit by a speeding car. He threw up on the ground. "You bitch ass nigga. I'ma kill you. I'ma kill you, Phoenix. I swear to God, I'ma kill you." He swore.

Phoenix knocked Ayesha's chair to the ground and unbound her. He threw her dress up and slid between her thighs. After unbuckling his pants, he slid into her in one smooth motion. He tossed her legs back and pounded her out in front of Tyson. "Aw shit. Aw shit. Fifteen years. Aw shit. Ayesha, baby." He fucked her as hard as he could.

Ayesha whimpered with her mouth wide open. Tears came out of her eyes. She'd been faithful to Tyson for so long. Now Phoenix had ruined it. He was thick and long. She felt him boring at her insides and couldn't help moaning from the feel of it? She dug her nails into his back and came.

Phoenix looked over at Tyson. "Grown man shit, nigga. Yo' bitch cumming. Tell him, bitch. What you doing? What you doing?"

"Unh. Uhhh. Cumming. I hate you. I hate you, Phoenix." She came and fell backward with Phoenix going to work on her.

Phoenix went full speed for five more minutes, and then pulled out. "Watch this shit, Tyson." He pumped himself and came all over Ayesha's face.

Tyson was going crazy trying to break his binds. "Aw, Phoenix, I'ma kill you." He promised.

Phoenix laughed. "We gon' see about that."

Chapter 16

Smoke hopped out of his black on black drop top Porsche and dusted the weed crumbs off of his lap. He took two last pulls from the Kush blunt that he was blowing, before he flicked it into the street. He walked around the back of the Porsche and opened the passenger's door for Precious to step out. She placed her black Jimmy Choo shoe on the pavement, and stood up, rocking a black and red Ferragamo shirt dress that highlighted her thick thighs, and ample backside. Smoke nodded his approval, as he looked around at the spectators that were watching them make their presence felt. He pulled his right pant leg over his red and black Balenciaga shoe that offset his matching Balenciaga fit. His neck was flooded with three good ropes sprayed in ice. The Patek on his left wrist was dripping in diamonds. He eyed the crowd through his Gucci frames, and held out his arm so that Precious could slide hers into his.

"You ready to roll inside, lil' mama?"

Precious nodded. She was overwhelmed by the amount of people waiting to get into Smoke's new night club. There were paparazzi taking pictures of them. They had to walk down the red carpet to get to the entrance of the establishment. She felt like a movie star. Smoke really was a major player in the game. She was really convinced now.

Smoke held her close while they walked down the red carpet. Cameras flashed. People were calling out to him. He ignored them and gave her all of his attention. "You see, shawty, this what it look like when you fucking wit' a true boss. All dem other niggas be pretending. This is real shit right hurr." He pulled her closer to him.

"I still can't believe that you waited to open Club Dynasty on my birthday. I think this is the best gift that I could have ever asked for." She felt emotional.

"What about dat wet diamond tennis bracelet you got on your left arm, or that Rollie wit' the pink diamonds in it that I got you? You sho me opening this club is better than all of them?" Smoke stopped and held her close while the paparazzi took a bunch of pictures of them.

"Just shows me that you care about me a lil' bit is all. I mean, I love my jewelry. Diamonds are a girl's best friend, of course, but I ain't chasing yo bag. I'm chasing your heart." She hugged him closer and allowed for the photographer to shoot them from a few different angles, before they kept walking.

"My shit cold as ice. I ain't got no good heart. If a mafucka wanna stay on top of this game, you leave that weak shit for the bitches. I'm a cold blooded boss. That's what I am, and that's what I will always be. You fuckin' wit' me, I'ma need you to leave that emotional shit for them other niggas. When you're in my presence, it's all about that ice box, and that money. Now mafuckas are looking at you and wondering who this bad bitch is that's on my arm. You be as stuck up as you can and make me look good. I could've chosen any other bitch to be here with tonight, but I chose you. That's a blessing from my behalf on the strength of you. You feel me, shawty?"

Precious nodded her head. "I do, and I got you."

"You better, or else I'ma spank that lil' ass tonight before I wax that mafucka. Now let's roll in here and show out. It's game time."

***

Eliza opened her eyes, and yawned. She stretched her arms above her head and kicked her legs down as far as they could go. Her bones popped. She closed her eyes back for a second. She heard Marsha moan, and then gasp loudly. She popped her eyes back open and sat up straight in the bed. She listened as best she could. Marsha moaned again. Greedy laughed. Eliza scooted out of the bed with her thighs wide open. She stood at the foot of the bed and listened carefully. Marsha began to moan louder and louder. She was saying something about it hurting a little bit. Eliza rushed into the living room.

Greedy pulled his piece all the way out of Marsha's ass, and slammed it back home. He had her bent over the couch, dogging her back door. He took a hold of her hips and pounded her out. "Tell me how it feels." He growled.

Marsha was in bliss. Greedy had screwed her in every hole that he could fit into, and by doing so, had completely turned her out. She didn't want to leave his sight. She was crazy about him.

Eliza ran full speed and pushed Greedy off of her friend. "Get off of her, Greedy. Damn."

Greedy fell backward and tripped over the coffee table. He landed on his back with his dick sticking straight up in the air. He was so high that his brain didn't register what had taken place for a few moments. Then he grew angry. "Eliza, what the fuck is wrong with you?"

"You're in here fucking her while I'm sleep. Why didn't you wake me up? What, you love this white bitch more than me now?" Eliza was close to tears.

Marsha crawled around on her knees. She was higher than Greedy. Greedy had given her two Percocet sixties, and a gram of the Rebirth. Marsha was lifted. Her sexual parts were screaming for more of Greedy. "Damn, Eliza, why are you hating, sis?"

"Because he is my man, bitch. You ain't supposed to be fucking him behind my back, but I guess that's the type of friend that you are, huh?" Eliza stood over her. She looked into her pink buttocks and saw how open her rosebud was? Her pussy dripped Greedy's seed. This infuriated Eliza. "Why, Greedy? Why? You said that I was your baby girl. Why would you want to screw her if I was laying right in the bed next to her? Why?"

Greedy stood up and tried to balance himself on his feet. He was so high off of the Rebirth that he couldn't think straight. "Shawty, who the fuck are you talking to like that?" He stepped forward and had to stop.

Eliza stepped up to him. "Do you love this bitch more than me, or am I still your baby? Tell me. Tell me right now." She demanded.

Greedy staggered backwards and struggled to open his eyes. The lean had him operating slowly. "I ain't gotta tell you shit." He slurred. "You the child, and I'm the man." He pointed to his chest.

Marsha stood up and walked over to him with her hand between her thighs. "Greedy, tell her to chill. Damn, chill, Eliza. We already didn't go home last night. We're both in trouble. When our parents get a hold of us, they are going to tear us a new one. We might as well have as much fun with him as we possibly can." She looked seductively at Greedy. "Ain't I right, Greedy?"

Greedy grabbed her by her ass and pulled her to him. "I heard you play volleyball and thangs. I always used to love watching them lil' white girls play volleyball. I used to only keep my eyes on this right here." He gripped Marsha's ass harder and slid his fingers into her groove. He found her open rosebud and sunk his middle finger into it.

Marsha was leaking from her kitten. "Mmm, let's finish."

Eliza covered her face. "Why are you two doing this to me? This is bullshit." She screamed.

Greedy frowned and moved Marsha out of his face. He walked toward Eliza with mounting anger. "Who the fuck you thank you talking to? Huh?"

Eliza backed away from him in fear. "Greedy, I just thought it should be me and you. I don't wanna share you no more. Marsha is trying to take you away from me, and I don't like it."

"Holy crap, Eliza, you're so fuckin' insecure. Don't you see what he's working with between his legs? Look at it. He can handle both of us. You're just going crazy for no reason. Get it together."

"Get it together. Bitch, don't tell me to get it together because you already have a boyfriend. Greedy is mine. Matter of fact, I'm sorry but you have to go." She started picking Marsha's clothes up off of the floor and throwing them at her.

"I'm not going anywhere. You don't run anything here. We're having a good time. You're the only one that is trying your best to ruin it. If anybody is leaving, it is undoubtedly you." Marsha snapped.

Greedy stood there nodding. His chin was to his chest. He snapped out of it and scratched the back of his neck. "You hoes chill."

Eliza was in Marsha's face. "You think you're running shit now? You think you're so pretty that you can take any boy from me. Is that it?"

Marsha rolled her eyes. "Wait, is this where I am supposed to be scared, or what?"

Eliza clenched her right fist as tight as she could get it. Then she cocked back and punched Marsha right in the nose, busting it. Eliza flew backward. "You scared now? Huh, bitch?"

Marsha caught her balance. Because of the drugs that she was on, her heart was beating so fast that it caused her blood to pour out of her like cherry Kool-Aid. "You slut, how dare you hit me." She balled up her fists and ran at Eliza full speed.

Eliza held a karate stance, waited until Marsha got close, and jumped in the air. She kicked her in the stomach, and round housed her into the wall, where Marsha bonked her forehead and fell out. She was knocked out cold.

Greedy looked down on her and busted up laughing. "Damn, this lil' bitch crazy as a muthafucka." He stood over Marsha. "Girl, get yo monkey ass up. She kicking yo ass."

Marsha struggled to come to her feet. She staggered, holding her stomach. "Why, Eliza? I thought you were my friend."

"How the fuck am I going to be your friend when you're creeping with my man while I'm sleep. It doesn't work like that." She hollered. "Now, pick up your shit and go."

Marsha nodded at her. "Okay, I'm out of here. You're a freaking psycho." She began to collect her articles of clothing.

Greedy sat on the arm of the couch. He was dazed and confused. "You hoes need to stop making all of that mafuckin' noise. Y'all blowing my high."

Marsha rushed to the front door with an arm full of her things. She threw it open and nearly bumped into Phoenix. He grabbed her by the throat with his right hand and pushed her back into the apartment. With his left hand, he aimed his silenced gun at Greedy and popped him twice. Poof. Poof.

The hot slugs knocked Greedy off of the couch, and to the floor. He hollered out in pain. "What the fuck?" He placed his hand over the shoulder wound that was leaking blood.

Eliza was frozen in place. She turned her head sideways when she recognized who the shooter was. "Phoenix, what's going on?"

Phoenix looked her scantily clad body over and licked his lips. "Eliza, get down on the ground." He rushed over and placed his foot on Greedy's chest. "So dis what you been on, huh?"

Greedy tried to move his foot off of him but had no success in doing so. "Bitch ass nigga, what you sweating me for? I ain't got no problems with you."

"Where is Smoke and that nigga Mikey? I ain't gon ask you too many more times, either. Where are they?"

"In their skin." He broke into a fit of laughter.

Marsha jumped up to make a run for the door. Phoenix aimed and popped her through the temple. Her head exploded on the right side. Before she fell to the ground, she was dead.

"You got jokes, right? Awright, cool. Brang her in."

Phoenix's body guard pushed Ayesha into the room. As soon as she saw the state of Eliza's undress, she became irate. She glared at Greedy. "She's only fifteen. She's fifteen, how dare you?" She rushed him kicking and stomping away at his body.

Greedy curled into a ball. "Get this dumb bitch off of me, Phoenix."

Phoenix loaded one bullet into his gun and cocked it so that it was in the chamber. He snatched Ayesha by the hair aggressively. "Huh, bitch. This mafucka got one in the chamber. Dump his bitch ass. Don't try shit stupid, either." He placed the barrel of his other gun to her head. "Kill him."

Ayesha didn't hesitate. She aimed the gun down at Greedy and got ready to pull the trigger. When Eliza came running full speed across the room yelling no. She tackled her mother. The gun went off. *Boom.* Ayesha fell to her back, and Eliza crawled away on her knees with a slug to her stomach. She coughed up blood and fell on her chest.

"Eliza, no. Baby." Ayesha jumped up.

Phoenix smoked evilly. He aimed and popped her twice in the jaw. She did a one-eighty, before falling to the ground holding her face. Phoenix stood over her and mugged her bleeding form. "No mercy, bitch." Poof. Poof. Poof. Ayesha's body jumped from the ground three times before life left her. Then he turned the gun on Eliza. He imagined his first infant son. He aimed the gun down at her as she crawled across the floor in agony. "Rest in peace, lil' Phoenix." Poof. Poof. Poof. All three bullets spit out of the silencer and tore massive chunks from the back of Eliza's head before she lay still in the middle of the carpet in death.

Greedy stood up laughing. He was delirious as the blood drained from him. "Fuck you, Phoenix. I ain't scared to go. Kill me, bitch nigga. Kill me right now."

Phoenix's henchman walked behind Greedy and punched him as hard as he could in the back of the head, knocking him out cold. He picked Greedy up and tossed him over his shoulder. "Trunk his ass, boss?"

"Yeah, put his bitch ass in the trunk. I got plans for him."

Chapter 17

Mikey stepped out into the hospital parking lot early Monday morning, with a blue doctor's mask over his face, and a brown paper bag full of medicine in his right hand. He still felt a bit sick, but the doctors had assured him that he was okay. His lungs felt like he was constantly inhaling little sharp pins, but the doctors had told him that the Coronavirus attacked his lungs. They'd said that the feeling should go away within a few weeks, and he was hopeful.

He coughed and tried to swallow his spit. His throat was so dry. "Mane, where the fuck is this girl at?" He asked out loud, looking both ways. He needed to sit down, his head began to pound.

As if on cue, Ivy rounded the corner of the parking lot in her twenty-twenty black on black Range Rover. She pulled in front of Mikey and popped the locks to the door. She was hoping that he wasn't in a foul mood. His last words to her before he had been quarantined was that he was going to kill her. She hoped that wasn't still on his mind.

Mikey opened the door and got into the truck. He pulled his seat belt across his body and clicked it into place. "What's up with you?"

"I'm good, how are you feeling?" Ivy was trying to feel him out. He looked angry, as he always did. His long dreadlocks were nappy, and all out of place.

"I'm feeling like I should kick yo' ass for having me admitted, and I would if they hadn't told me that you saved my life. Next time, when I tell yo ratchet ass to do somethin', you listen to me, no matter the stakes. Do you understand that?"

"Yeah, I do, and you're welcome. I mean, if I wouldn't have done what I did, you wouldn't have been around to curse me out. Have you stopped to think about that?" She pulled out of the parking lot.

"That doesn't mean shit, Ivy, you're my bitch, and when I tell yo' ass to do something, you do it. You don't pick and choose what orders to follow, and which ones not to follow. Shit don't work like that."

Ivy kept rolling. "Okay, next time I will just do what you say and not even think about how much I care about you." She shook her head in anger. "Anyway, you couldn't have gotten out of there at a better time. Memphis is going to shit, and the lil so called hustlers that you left out here to make those major moves for you ain't on nothin'. They were getting popped up, and robbed, left and right. It's ridiculous."

Mikey sat up in his seat. "What are you talking about? I ain't been down more than a month. How the fuck could shit fall off that much?"

She shrugged her shoulders. "I promise you, I don't know, but it's all bad. I'm just glad that you are home, and now we can get things back on track."

"You're right about that." Mikey pulled down the sun visor to block the harsh glare of the sun that was shining into his eyes, giving him a headache. He looked over the streets of Memphis while she drove. It felt like he was just getting out of prison, and in a sense, he kind of was. "What about my money? You were on top of my ends?"

"The few dope boys that are still loyal to you have been paying up. I stacked about a hundred gees for you since you were gone."

"A hundred gees, bitch, are you kidding me? That ain't no mafuckin' money. You're saying we've been only pulling in twenty five gees a week? Really?"

"Please don't take this shit out on me. I told you that there are just a few dope boys that have been hitting you when they were supposed to. The few others that probably were looking to remain loyal to you were either shot up by those Duffle Bag Cartel thugs, or they were shot up by the Bread Gang, and robbed. Smoke, and his crew, are out here running wild. This shit is madness. Oh, but then again, they just found the bodies of Tyson's wife and daughter, so I am thinking that somebody is even targeting the Bread Gang."

"The Bread Gang, who the fuck is that? These niggas came out in just the few weeks I been down?"

"It's been more than a month, and yes. Smoke is their leader, and them fools, Greedy and Tyson were right behind him. I don't know what's up now, though, because ain't nobody heard from Smoke, Tyson, or Greedy. They ain't been on Facebook or none of that. I think Phoenix might be roaming through this bitch like the grim reaper."

"You mean to tell me that he ain't dead?" Mikey snapped.

"Not as far as I know, he ain't." Ivy pulled onto the expressway.

Suddenly the migraine that was flirting with Mikey came full-fledged. There was a pouncing sensation right behind his eyes. He rubbed his temples. "It's all good. I'ma figure this shit out. I always do. I should've known that Smoke was a snake, and I should've killed Phoenix when I had the chance, on multiple occasions. All of this derives from my fuck ups, but it's good, though." He continued to rub his temples. "What about the good news? Do you have any of that?"

Ivy shook her head. "As sad as it is to say it, I really don't. Shit has been haywire since you were gone, and I only hope that you can get it all back on track without becoming a victim out here in these streets. I still love yo black ass."

Mikey was in no mood to be lovey dovey. He was heated. If Ivy had only stacked a hundred thousand dollars while he was away, then that meant that he only had a little more than a million dollars to his name. In his mind, he was broke. There was no way that a true boss could run a major organization with only a million dollars to his name. He was so angry that he wanted to punch somebody. "So which one of my trap hoods been the most loyal?"

"Black Haven, baby. The Projects. The mafuckas over there, despite their adversity, have been making shit happen. Everybody still holds you up like you're the king of Black Haven. You gotta be grateful for that."

"And what about the Mound?" Orange Mound was his first homeland. He was born and bred there. "Who are they honoring harder than anybody else?"

"Well, you already know that Memphis belongs to the legacy of Taurus as a whole. The Orange Mound is no different. If you roll through there, you'll see all kinds of pictures of Taurus painted on the walls, because his birthday was just on April the twenty-seventh. But after him, they are hollering Smoke. They say that Smoke is the king of Orange Mound, and he's taking that shit to the head. At least, I think he is. Ain't nobody see him in a few days."

Mikey grunted. "Yeah, we're about to see all of that. Roll me to a few of the traps and let me collect some of my bread so I can show these niggas that I am alive and well. After I connect a few loose ends, I see I got some heads to bust, so that'll be priority number two. But for now, let's roll, baby. We got a lot of work to do."

"Cool, Mikey, you already know I'm riding wit' you until the bitter end." Ivy stepped on the gas.

***

Natalia opened the front door to her mansion and took a step back. "Please come in and thank you for coming."

Alicia slowly walked inside with her Birkin bag in her hand. She side eyed Natalia and kept walking. "I'm still trying to figure out why you couldn't tell me what was good over the phone. Why do you need for me to come and holler at you in person?"

Natalia closed the door to the mansion and locked it. "As a woman, I feel like there is a bit of animosity between you and I, and I just want to get a nice understanding with you. That way, we can go on with our lives. So if you don't mind, I have prepared a nice steak dinner with all of the fixings, got out a bottle of aged wine from the early nineteen hundreds collection, Phoenix is out of town, and Sabrina has both the baby and Shante. We are free to be grownups and to speak freely. So you can say whatever you feel, and it's all good."

"Awright, I think that you are a petty bitch for naming your son after mine. You knew that my son was supposed to be Phoenix's junior, and because those whack jobs took him away from me, you hijacked his name. You are a petty bitch, and that's how I feel."

"Okay, I see that we are kicking this off quite early. Well, Alicia, if that's how you really feel, I think that you are a straight slut, and Phoenix would never have been in this position if you would've known how to keep your legs closed. You are a whore, and I don't give a fuck what you wanted to name your child, I'ma name mine after his father, and my future husband."

"Bitch, that is your cousin, and if you ever do try to marry him, they are going to lock yo stupid ass up. That ain't happening. And since you think I'ma a slut, I'ma just tell you what I think of you."

"Will you, now?" Natalia crossed her arms. "Well, let me hear this."

"Bitch, you are an incest queen. Your self-esteem is so low that you gotta fuck wit' a nigga in yo family, just because you already know another nigga would dog yo' yellow ass. You're mixed, and you still ain't all that. I can guarantee you bought that ass and those thick lips you got on your face. That shit ain't real. But I guess when you get a hold of the right amount of cash, you can be whatever you wanna be."

Now Natalia was offended. "Everything on me is real. It either comes from my mother." She pulled on her long hair and pointed to her crystal blue eyes. "Or it comes from my father's side of the family." She hoisted up her breasts and smacked her fat ass. It jiggled. "And with all of that weave in your head, you should be the last one to talk about what's real, and what's fake, because all of your shit is fake."

Alicia stepped into her face. "You think that you're all of that, don't you?"

Natalia smiled. "You have no idea all of what I really am. If you knew who you were standing in front of, you would bow down and honor me. I am that bitch. Trust and believe I was that way before Lizzo."

"Bitch, change yo' son's name. I'm not playing wit' you."

"Fuck you. Kiss my mixed ass."

Slap.

Alicia slapped her as hard as she could and tackled her to the ground. "Change that baby name. Phoenix Jr. was my son." She got ready to punch Natalia in the face.

Natalia rolled her off of her and hopped up. She dabbed her finger to the corner of her mouth and looked at the blood there. She spit it on the carpet. "That was the last time that you ever put your hands on me." She pulled a serrated knife from the small of her back.

Alicia took a step back and looked for a weapon. "Bitch, why you gotta pull out a blade and shit? What, you're scared to throw these thangs?" She pulled the lamp from the table and held it up, before yanking the cord out of the wall.

Natalia placed her ass length hair into a knot and rolled her head around on her shoulder. "One of us is not about to leave this room alive. Unlike you, I got a child to live for, so I plan on making it out on the other side. She rushed Alicia at full speed and jumped in the air. She slammed the knife into the upper portion of her shoulder and twisted it.

"Arrrrghhh." Alicia screamed at the top of her lungs.

Natalia took the knife out and swept Alicia's feet from under her with a floor round house. Alicia fell, and she rolled on top of her. She smacked her with her right hand and slammed the knife into her shoulder again. Alicia wailed, leaned up and head butt Natalia off of her. Natalia could feel the blood pouring out of her nose. She laughed and stood up. Alicia pulled the knife out of her shoulder and held it as a weapon.

Natalia laughed. "You sure you're ready to fight until the death? Huh, bitch? You better remember that I have two legacies that war constantly inside of my blood. There is the crazy Russian blood that seeks to conquer the world. It is cold. It is calculating. It is relentless, and smart. Then there is my father Taurus's blood. It is unforgiving. It is savage. It is merciless. She stepped into the kitchen and grabbed a machete from the pantry that she'd hidden there. The metal blade shined in the kitchen light. She stepped back into the living room. "Are you ready, Alicia?"

Alicia looked her over with hatred. "You muthafuckin' right, I am." Alicia took off running toward Natalia with the knife in her hand. She raised it over her head. She fixed her eyes on Natalia's chest. She saw herself plunging the knife deep into Natalia. But before she could plant it, Natalia side stepped her, and swung the Machete with all of her might. It slammed into the base of Alicia's throat and cut into the meat there.

Alicia felt like she'd been hit in the throat by an axe. She choked and dropped her knife. Her hands went to her bleeding neck. She struggled to get up.

Natalia circled her. "This is for mother Russia." She swung the Machete and sliced a huge chunk out of Alicia's neck, knocking Alicia to the ground. She walked closer. "Get up, bitch? Talk that bullshit now."

Whack.

The blade opened Alicia so much that blood was spurting everywhere like a geyser. Natalia became excited by the blood. She raised the Machete and brought it down again, and then again. She became giddy whacking Alicia over and over. "Die, bitch. Die."

Alicia jumped up and tried her best to run to the front door. Natalia ran behind her and sliced the back of her neck skeeting blood across the couch and the paintings on the wall. Alicia fell to her knees. She placed her hand over the large wound. Blood seeped through her fingers and dripped off of her wrist and elbow. "Why? Why are you doing this to me?" She stumbled and stood up with her shirt drenched in her own blood. Her eyes crossed. She was lightheaded.

Natalia walked up on her with the machete dripping. "Any woman that Phoenix loves will meet this fate. There is no room in his heart for anybody other than me. I am for him only."

A line of blood squirted from Alicia's neck. She grew weak in the knees. "You can have him. I don't want him. Please just let me get to a hospital. I will never fuck with y'all again." She fell to her knees, woozy.

"In Russia, we finish what we started. You are prey. Die, bitch, and say hi to your son for me. Here is a secret, I paid to

146

have your ugly son killed, and it was the delight of my life."
She laughed for a moment, then her eyes turned low and menacing. She raised the machete to finish Alicia.

"You bitch." With one last burst of energy Alicia hopped from the floor and tackled Natalia into the China cabinet shattering it. Games popped into the air and settled around both of their bodies. Alicia landed on top of Natalia and punched her three times with her bloody fist. She became too weak to finish her.

Natalia screamed and swung the Machete with all of her might. It lodged itself into Alicia's neck so far that blood ran out of her throat like a broken faucet. She died before her head hit the hardwood floor. Natalia slid from under her and stomped her face. "Only I will mother Phoenix's son." Her chest heaved up and down. She called her clean up men to dispose of Alicia's body, and then jumped in the shower with a sadistic smile on her face.

Ghost

Chapter 18

Smoke walked through the State Fair Grounds with his arm around Precious. He kissed her cheek and kept strolling. It was a hot and humid day, and the Tennessee State Fair was crowded and jumping. Smoke had already won Precious two huge stuffed animals, and was thinking about winning her a third, even though she was having a hard time carrying the ones that she had. She was growing on him as a woman. He felt himself becoming enamored by her, and for some unforeseen reason, he didn't want her out of his presence.

He kissed her cheek again as he navigated her through the crowd of people. "Baby, are you enjoying yourself?"

Precious nodded. "Yeah, this joint lit. I feel like I ain't never had this much fun. Thank you for bringing me out, and for spending so much time wit' me, Smoke. I know you are a very busy man and you could've been anywhere else, but you're here with me. I appreciate that." She kissed his cheek.

"Long as you know who daddy is." He smiled and held her tighter within his embrace.

"I do, and he lived back in Houston." She snickered.

"Aw, that's how you gon' do me?"

"That's just how I'm gon' do you. We might be kicking it a lil' bit, but you ain't reached that daddy status just yet. I keep waiting for you to turn on me and go back to the ways that everybody and they mama that know you say you gon' go back to. I mean, it's been lovely so far, but you're sure that once I give you this lil' kitty, that you aren't going to turn on me?"

Smoke flared his nostrils. "Shawty, what I tell you about listening to other niggas? Didn't I tell you that shit like that will ruin us fast? Now you need to rock wit' me the long way and judge me off of how I carry myself every single day. Fuck everybody else. Everybody else ain't flying to Dubai wit' me at the end of the week, are they?"

She shook her head. "Not that I know of."

"Aiight den. Fuck wit' me." He gripped her ass and pulled her closer to him.

Precious hugged his waist. "So what else is on our agenda for today? Are we just going to keep playing games until I get too many stuffed animals to carry, or are we going to go back to your place, and you can finally buss me down? I think I might be feenin' for you." She batted her eyelashes. "And I mean, you have earned it."

Smoke gripped her ass a little harder, imagining what it would be like to finally fuck Precious. He'd been so close over the last few weeks but had decided to back off to see if he could have enough discipline to treat her differently than what he had treated every other female before. It was driving him insane because Precious was so bad to him, especially physically. And even though she was only eighteen years old, she carried herself like a true boss. He liked that.

"Look at you being all excited." She laughed. "So do you wanna get out of here right now, or what?"

"Let's grab a slice first, and then we'll bounce." He guided her to the pizza stand and stood in a lengthy line.

Precious stood in front of him and backed up so that her ass was on his front. "Have you decided what you're going to make me yet? I was thinking of a bottle girl. I know they are saying that you have to be twenty-one to handle the liquor, but ain't nobody gonna be all up in our business like that. If I was a bottle girl, I would be able to promote the club in such a way with class and elegance. I also know how to be flirtatious, and how to give the club just that overall feeling of sexy. The stripper thing is cool, but after you get a hold of this gap you ain't gon want me grinding all up on other men. Besides, what would make me so special to you after that, if I did do that? Niggas would be looking at you like you're stupid."

"Fuck would they be doing that for?" He moved them forward in the line.

"Because they would know how all of this ass feel, and they would be able to pay to see what your woman feels like back there. Niggas be doing that shit just to live in your shoes for a minute. You know how that shit go." She looked up at him. "I'm my daddy's girl. I don't want nobody touching on me, but you. That's just how I feel."

Smoke tensed his muscles and became seriously possessive of her. "Well, you damn sure ain't about to be stripping for nobody other than me. So you can get that shit out of your mind." He stepped up to the window, and ordered them two slices of pizza, paid for it, and was handed the food. He gave her one and took the other. They walked away from the window.

"My girl just sent me a screenshot of that Black Haven nigga Mikey's Rolls Royce Phantom. I guess he's back in Memphis, and everywhere he is rolling, he got like three vans following him. This screenshot was in North Memphis. I heard you used to fuck wit' him but y'all are beefing now. What's good wit' that?"

"Shit happens. Fuck that nigga. If he rolls around through the city now, then it's time for his sucka ass to get smoked. Pun intended." Smoke felt himself becoming heated. "Come on, let's roll out to my pad so I can see what my baby is working wit'." He dropped his pizza to the ground, and took the teddy bears out of her hands.

***

Phoenix stepped into the basement and placed a pair of black latex gloves on his hands. He took a pair of pliers out of the tool box and stepped up to a sleeping Tyson. Tyson's face was swollen from the constant ass whooping that he'd received from Phoenix and his cold hearted henchmen. Phoenix slapped Tyson across the face and jarred him awake. "Wake yo punk ass up."

Tyson awoke hollering into the duct tape. His eyes were blackened. Sweat and blood ran down his face. He began to shake like crazy.

"Lil' nigga, Ayesha is dead. Eliza is dead. And some lil' white girl with blonde hair is dead. Greedy was fuckin' the shit out of your daughter, if that's your daughter. And well, the shit hit the fan. It is what it is. Have you spoken to Greedy since he was chained next to you?"

Tyson shook his head. He hollered into the tape in emotional agony. He didn't know if what Phoenix was saying was the truth, but if it were, it was devastating news. He couldn't imagine himself not being able to be with Ayesha anymore, or Eliza. They were both his world, despite the looming paternity of Eliza.

Phoenix snatched the duct tape off of his mouth. "Fuck you trying to say?"

"Come on, Phoenix, man. Please tell me that you didn't kill my family. Please, man. Tell me what type of dirty game you're playing? Those were my babies." He cried.

"Hands down, you the ugliest crying nigga I ever seen. Yo' face all wrinkled and shit. Dawg cut that shit out because I feel nothing. Straight up. Yo' people dead. Yo bitch and my god daughter. Oh well, he was fucking Eliza. That lil' bitch was naked as hell when I got there. Mmm. Her body was righteous, too. What a waste."

Tyson looked over to Greedy. "You was fucking my daughter, bitch ass nigga?"

Phoenix ripped the tape off of Greedy's mouth as well. "Respond, nigga."

"Don't act like you ain't thought about fuckin' that lil' bitch, too. She walked around with her lil' fresh ass poked all the way out, with them fat ass titties. Nipples all big and shit. Hell yeah, I fucked on multiple occasions." He closed his eyes. "Best pussy I ever had, too? I got no regrets, other than this shit. Caught a nigga slipping wit' his pants down. Fuck."

"She was fifteen, nigga. Fifteen. What the fuck is wrong with you?" Tyson snapped.

"Well I grew her lil' ass up quick. She came to me a virgin and inexperienced as a muthafucka. It was so cute, but by the time she left me, she was riding me and taking the dick. Eating pussy and every thang. Damn, that was my lil' bitch." Greedy started to get hard from just thinking about it.

Tyson went crazy within his binds. He yanked at the chains that held his wrists in place. "I'ma kill you Greedy. You bitch ass nigga. You ain't nothing but a predator. That's it. A low life, hype ass predator."

Greedy shrugged his shoulders. "I like coochie, nigga. Every man in the world likes coochie. I just stick to young hoes, I can't help it. Bury me a predator den." He closed his eyes.

"Tyson, since I really don't think you had much to do with my son's death, I'm going to do you a favor." Phoenix knelt down and picked up two small axes with long handles. He took them and set them on the table.

"Oh yeah, what are you going to do for me, Phoenix?" Tyson mugged him, and then the axes.

"I'm finna let you get your revenge on Greedy. I'ma give you an axe, and I'ma let you beat his ass to death with it." Phoenix snickered.

"What? That shit ain't fair. I ain't kill yo baby, either. That shit ain't have nothing to do with me." Greedy was nervous.

"Y'all already know I don't like neither one of you bitch ass niggas. So, Greedy, I'ma give you one, too. You get to fuck him up, as well. The last man standing will get a surprise." Phoenix motioned for his huge bodyguards to come and release one of each of Tyson and Greedy's hands. Once they were released an axe was placed into it, but the bodyguard held the hand until Phoenix backed away. "Now you niggas are side by side, it's even. One of you will die, good luck. Release they bitch ass."

As soon as the guards moved, Greedy swung his axe and planted it directly into Tyson's chest. It got stuck and crushed his breastplate. Tyson hollered like a wounded wolf. He swung his axe and slammed it into Greedy's ear. The blade cut through the side of his face. He refused to holler, even though he was in excruciating pain. He yanked his axe out of Tyson's chest, and swung it again. This time it connected with Tyson's forehead and killed him immediately. He pulled it out, and swung it again, and again. Then he dropped the axe, breathing hard.

Phoenix nodded. "Now that's how you kill a mafucka." Phoenix took his head and slammed it with all of his might into the brick wall behind him over and over again with a scowl on his face. He slammed it until the back of his head flattened, and the life left out of Greedy. Then he stepped back. "Two down, two to go."

***

154

Natalia tossed and turned inside of the King sized bed. She kept having one nightmare after the next, and she felt hotter than usual. She kicked the blankets off of her body and set up in bed. There was a constant knocking on her front door. She got out of the bed and wrapped her robe around her body. She took her .9 millimeter from under her pillow and made haste to the front door. She checked the security cameras and saw the back of a large figure standing at her door. She cocked her gun and pulled the door open. She was about to raise the pistol and place it into the man's face when suddenly his eyes became familiar. He pulled his hood back.

"Daddy? Is that you?" She felt her stomach flip over twice.

Taurus held a finger to his lips and nodded. "Baby girl, they know that I am alive now. You are in danger. We need to talk." He stepped inside, along with four masked Jamaican assassins, and took ahold of her into his arms.

Natalia hugged him and began to cry. "Okay, daddy. Let's talk. Thank you, God. Let's talk."

Chapter 19

Precious stepped into the bedroom and pulled open her red satin Victoria's Secret sheer robe. She looked across the room at Smoke as he dropped his Ferragamo pants and stepped out of them. He took his pistol and hid it under the pillow that he was going to lay his head on, then stood and eyed Precious from across the room.

Precious closed the bedroom door and licked her succulent lips. "You think you're ready for me, daddy?"

Smoke stepped out of his boxers and grabbed ahold of his piece. "Since the first day I met you. Now bring yo lil fine ass here and let me see what that thang is about." He walked over to her.

Precious met him in the center of the room, beside the bed, she wrapped her arms around his neck, and kissed all over his lips. "You better take it easy on me. Mmm. You know this is my first time." She kissed him some more.

Smoke squeezed her ass and rubbed all over it. It felt soft, and hefty to the touch. He bit her neck. "I'm from the Orange Mound, shawty, we don't never take it easy on nobody." He bit into her neck and picked her up. He threw her on the bed and climbed between her thighs. His hand went right between her legs. He felt her hot, squishy sex lips. The cloth was already damp. This made him shiver. "Damn, boo."

Precious licked all over his lips. Taste me, daddy. Please, I need you to taste me."

Smoke climbed out of the bed and stood back. His four gold ropes swung around on his neck. "We finna do this shit like we supposed too. I'm finna make yo' first time the best time and get on that boss shit wit' you." He left out of her sight and went into the closet. After moving back to the wall he pulled out two duffle bags of cash that he had yet to count. He took one stuffed bag and dumped the money on top of Precious. Then he picked up the other and did the same thing. Five hundred thousand dollars in cash fell all over her and the bed. He climbed back on top of her, and forced her knees backward exposing her pussy through the panties. He kissed the juicy lips. "Now we finna get on that shit, shawty." He pulled the material to the side and began to eat her like a savage.

Precious yelped and began to moan loudly. "Uhhhh shit. Shit, Smoke. Uhhhh, daddy." She felt Smoke licking in between her folds hungrily. He took a hold of her clit and twirled his tongue around it. This sent tremors throughout her body. She began to gasp over and over. His tongue went deeply into her, and she jumped into it.

Smoke inhaled her scent, and it drove him wild. He flicked his tongue faster and faster. He felt her tense up. "Un-huh. Un-huh. Cum, bitch. Cum." He nibbled on her clit and sucked on it.

Precious hollered and came hard. "Aw shit, daddy. Aw shit. Ooo-a." She fell back on the bed.

Smoke kissed her pussy one last time, and then he got between her thighs. He rubbed her slit. "I'm finna buss this shit down. You already know that you're my baby. It's been a long time coming." He grabbed his piece and began to work the head into her sex lips.

Precious moaned and grabbed the gun from under the pillow. She cocked it nonchalantly and brought it out and aimed it at Smoke. "Get yo bitch ass off of me." *Boom.*

The bullet smacked into Smoke's chest and knocked him backward. He fell to the floor completely taken off guard. His eyes were bucked. He placed his hand over the gunshot wound to make sure that it was indeed there. "Fuck." He was dazed. He used the bed to stand up.

Precious threw her dress over her head, and mugged Smoke. "Daddy, I told you this nigga was a goofy."

Mikey slid into the room laughing. "Turn coat ass nigga. One way you can always get a mafucka to slip is by use of a bitch's pussy. This shit is hilarious. Look at all of this money. My mafuckin' money. Simple ass nigga."

Precious came over to Mikey and kissed his lips. "What do you want me to do?"

Mikey moved her to the side. "Nigga step yo ass out of this room, you're bleeding all over my money. I don't like that."

Smoke was struggling to breathe. The bullet that entered into him had pierced his left lung. "Fuck you, Mikey." He took a deep breath.

Mikey shook his head. "N'all, it ain't no fuck me, Smoke, you can't do that. Just like you can't fuck my bitch. Yous a goofy."

Precious came forward and aimed her gun. "Let me smoke this fool, daddy. Let me show him that we get down in Houston, just like they get down out here in Memphis. But the women run Houston, its time niggas realize that shit, too."

Houston was set to be Mikey's new stomping grounds. He'd made a lot of connections out that way. One of the major connections being Rivera himself. Rivera had given him the low down on Smoke, and Mikey used it to his benefit. Mikey stepped up to Smoke. "Where is Phoenix?"

Smoke was woozy. "Fuck you, and fuck Phoenix. Fuck both of you niggas." He harked and spit directly into Mikey's face.

Precious sidestepped Mikey and finger fucked her trigger. "Nasty ass nigga." *Boom. Boom. Boom. Boom.*

Smoke took the bullets and ran past them with Precious on his ass. *Boom.* Another bullet hit his back. *Boom.* Another his right arm. *Boom.* Another popped the back of his neck and turned him around. Precious jumped up and kicked him in the chest. He flew backward.

She pressed the barrel to his forehead. "Gang. Gang." *Boom. Boom. Boom.*

His brains blew out the back of his head. A puddle of blood formed around him. He jerked on the carpet. His body guards stood around him as the life dissipated from his body. They looked up at Mikey who they honored as their rightful leader of the Duffle Bag Cartel.

Mikey looked down on Smoke's body. "You muthafuckas pay attention because this is what disloyalty looks like. Clear this bitch out. Every ounce of my money in here, get it, and let's go. We're out of here in five minutes." He pulled Precious to him and tongued her down.

***

"Natalia." Shante ran into the mansion and wrapped her arms around Natalia's waist. She hugged her tightly. "I missed you so much." The light from the sun coming through the window reflected off of Shante's forehead. She smiled up at Natalia. "Where is my brother? Can I see him?"

Natalia nodded her head. "You sure can baby. He's upstairs in the nursery. Gon on up, there is somebody up there that wants to meet you anyway." She spoke in terms of her father, Taurus.

"Okay." She hugged Natalia again, and headed upstairs to the nursery.

Natalia smiled until Shante got to the top of the stairs, and then her face turned to a scowl. She stepped on to the brick porch, and eyed Sabrina, sitting in her Lexus truck, scrolling down the call log of her phone. Instead of calling out to her, she stepped back into the mansion and grabbed her Chanel bag. She went back outside and opened Sabrina's truck door. She placed the Chanel bag on the floor under the seat. "Hey girl, what you doing?"

"I'm just finishing this last text." Sabrina was answering the last questions from Kevin in regards to the federal investigation that was being launched by his department. So far she had made sure that she hadn't left anything out. Kevin had made it perfectly clear that it was in her best interest to tell the department everything that they needed to know in regards to Phoenix's crimes, and the operations of the Duffle Bag Cartel. She did what she could, and she prayed that it was enough to keep her from being indicted for whatever reason.

"Oh, anyway, I just wanted to come down and say hi. Thank you for keeping an eye on Shante. I know she has been keeping you busy. I should be able to keep my eye on her from here on out. I don't want her around no snitch anyway." Natalia glared at her.

Sabrina was in mid text. She froze when she heard those words. She looked over to Natalia. "Snitch? What are you talking about?"

"Nothin', I'm just playin' wit' you girl. Well, I betta get back in here. I'll see bits of you later." She climbed out of the truck and closed the door.

"You'll see bits of me later? What does that mean?" Sabrina hollered out of the window.

"It's a Russian term. Don't worry about it." Natalia jogged into the mansion and eyed Sabrina before she closed the door.

Sabrina started the ignition and pulled out of the driveway. She waited until she was out of the gated community before she called Kevin's direct number. He picked up on the fourth ring. "Kevin, I think Natalia may be on to me. She called me a snitch." She hollered into the phone.

"Impossible, there is no way that she could possibly know that you are working with us. The investigation has been held tightly to all of our chests." He assured her.

"Well, something doesn't seem right. Her exact words were she didn't want Shante hanging around with a snitch."

Kevin was quiet for a moment. "Those were the words she used?"

"Exactly. What do you think that means?" Sabrina entered on the freeway and picked up speed.

"It sounds like it means you're screwed."

"What?" Sabrina felt her heart skip a beat.

"The life of a snitch is always temporary." He hollered in Russian.

Sabrina looked down at her phone. "But you said..."

Boom.

The Lexus truck blew into a ball of fire and shot into the air, where it separated into a bunch of little pieces. They sailed to the ground on fire. The cars on the expressway swerved around them. Some crashed, trying to avoid the blaze, while others escaped with no injury.

***

Natalia took her thumb off of the detonation device and laughed. She could see the black cloud in the sky ten miles out. She knew it was Sabrina. She wired the hundred thousand dollars into Kevin's offshore account and closed the door to her mansion. "All that Phoenix loved before me will perish." She whispered.

***

Mikey grabbed the last duffle bag and tossed it to his head of security. The goon took the bag and stuffed it, along with the others, into the black van that was headed to Houston, Texas, where Mikey was going to reassemble and reestablish the new Duffle Bag Cartel. The van had a total of six million dollars in cash. For Mikey that was a good start for a new location.

He'd already staked his claim to a few of the project buildings in Clover Land. They were in need of quality narcotics and his plug with Rivera was going to make sure that he kept both Memphis and Houston on lock. All of Smoke's crew had switched over to him, and Black Haven's goons pledged their allegiance to him as well. All in all, Mikey was certain that it was impossible for him to lose, especially since the Duffle Bag Cartel had two judges, and a senator on the payroll.

Ivy came beside him and kissed his neck. "I'm so happy. We can finally leave Memphis alone for a little while. Things are going to be so much better in Houston." She kissed his neck again and loaded into his Range Rover.

Mikey cheesed as he watched his workers getting everything in position to travel. When they were done, they stood in place, looking for his next command. Mikey liked that power. He held his hand up. "Everybody, let's go. Houston is the next stop."

***

Mikey and the Duffle Bag Cartel members that he was relocating to the Houston chapter arrived in Houston five hours later. Mikey pulled the Range Rover into a rundown Clover Land Project building and nodded his head when he saw fifty members of the Duffle Bag Cartel already waiting in the parking lot for him. He could feel the excitement of the power flowing through his veins. He snickered. "This that shit I'm talking about right here. You see dis shit, baby?" He continued to look over the animals that were crowding around his truck.

Ivy reached under the seat and grabbed the Mach Uzi. She slammed it to the side of his head. "Yous a dumb ass nigga."

Mikey held his hands up. "What the fuck is you doing?"

Phoenix stepped through the crowd of Duffle Bag Cartel killas and slid the shotgun to Mikey's temple. "Bitch nigga, you could never run my shit. I am the Duffle Bag Cartel king. Rest in blood, nigga."

Boom.

The End

Submission Guideline

Submit the first three chapters of your completed manuscript to ldpsubmissions@gmail.com, subject line: Your book's title. The manuscript must be in a .doc file and sent as an attachment. Document should be in Times New Roman, double spaced and in size 12 font. Also, provide your synopsis and full contact information. If sending multiple submissions, they must each be in a separate email.

Have a story but no way to send it electronically? You can still submit to LDP/Ca$h Presents. Send in the first three chapters, written or typed, of your completed manuscript to:

LDP: Submissions Dept
Po Box 870494
Mesquite, Tx 75187

DO NOT send original manuscript. Must be a duplicate.

Provide your synopsis and a cover letter containing your full contact information.

Thanks for considering LDP and Ca$h Presents.

Coming Soon from Lock Down Publications/Ca$h Presents

BOW DOWN TO MY GANGSTA

By **Ca$h**

TORN BETWEEN TWO

By **Coffee**

THE STREETS STAINED MY SOUL **II**

By **Marcellus Allen**

BLOOD OF A BOSS **VI**

SHADOWS OF THE GAME II

By **Askari**

LOYAL TO THE GAME **IV**

By **T.J. & Jelissa**

A DOPEBOY'S PRAYER **II**

By **Eddie "Wolf" Lee**

IF LOVING YOU IS WRONG… **III**

By **Jelissa**

TRUE SAVAGE **VII**

MIDNIGHT CARTEL III

DOPE BOY MAGIC III

By **Chris Green**

BLAST FOR ME **III**

A SAVAGE DOPEBOY III

By **Ghost**

A HUSTLER'S DECEIT III

KILL ZONE **II**

BAE BELONGS TO ME III

SOUL OF A MONSTER III

By **Aryanna**

THE COST OF LOYALTY **III**

By **Kweli**

CHAINED TO THE STREETS II

By **J-Blunt**

KING OF NEW YORK V

COKE KINGS IV

BORN HEARTLESS IV

By **T.J. Edwards**

GORILLAZ IN THE BAY V

De'Kari

THE STREETS ARE CALLING II

Duquie Wilson

KINGPIN KILLAZ IV

STREET KINGS III

PAID IN BLOOD III

CARTEL KILLAZ IV

Hood Rich

SINS OF A HUSTLA II

ASAD

TRIGGADALE III

Elijah R. Freeman

KINGZ OF THE GAME V

Playa Ray

SLAUGHTER GANG IV

RUTHLESS HEART III

By Willie Slaughter

THE HEART OF A SAVAGE II

By Jibril Williams

FUK SHYT II

By Blakk Diamond

THE DOPEMAN'S BODYGAURD II

By Tranay Adams

TRAP GOD II

By Troublesome

YAYO III

A SHOOTER'S AMBITION II

By S. Allen

GHOST MOB

Stilloan Robinson

KINGPIN DREAMS II

By Paper Boi Rari

CREAM

By Yolanda Moore

SON OF A DOPE FIEND II

By Renta

FOREVER GANGSTA II

By Adrian Dulan

LOYALTY AIN'T PROMISED II

By Keith Williams

THE PRICE YOU PAY FOR LOVE II

By Destiny Skai

THE LIFE OF A HOOD STAR

By Rashia Wilson

TOE TAGZ III

By Ah'Million

CONFESSIONS OF A GANGSTA II

By Nicholas Lock

PAID IN KARMA II

By **Meesha**

I'M NOTHING WITHOUT HIS LOVE II

By Monet Dragun

CAUGHT UP IN THE LIFE II

By Robert Baptiste

NEW TO THE GAME II

By **Malik D. Rice**

Life of a Savage II

By **Romell Tukes**

Quiet Money II

By **Trai'Quan**

Available Now

RESTRAINING ORDER **I & II**

By **CA$H & Coffee**

LOVE KNOWS NO BOUNDARIES **I II & III**

By **Coffee**

RAISED AS A GOON I, II, III & IV

BRED BY THE SLUMS I, II, III

Ghost

BLAST FOR ME I & II

ROTTEN TO THE CORE I II III

A BRONX TALE I, II, III

DUFFEL BAG CARTEL I II III IV

HEARTLESS GOON I II III IV

A SAVAGE DOPEBOY I II

HEARTLESS GOON I II III

DRUG LORDS I II III

By **Ghost**

LAY IT DOWN **I & II**

LAST OF A DYING BREED

BLOOD STAINS OF A SHOTTA I & II III

By **Jamaica**

LOYAL TO THE GAME I II III

LIFE OF SIN I, II III

By **TJ & Jelissa**

BLOODY COMMAS I & II

SKI MASK CARTEL I II & III

KING OF NEW YORK I II,III IV

RISE TO POWER I II III

COKE KINGS I II III

BORN HEARTLESS I II III

By **T.J. Edwards**

IF LOVING HIM IS WRONG…I & II

LOVE ME EVEN WHEN IT HURTS I II III

By **Jelissa**

WHEN THE STREETS CLAP BACK I & II III

By **Jibril Williams**

A DISTINGUISHED THUG STOLE MY HEART I II & III

LOVE SHOULDN'T HURT I II III IV

RENEGADE BOYS I II III IV

PAID IN KARMA

By **Meesha**

A GANGSTER'S CODE I &, II III

A GANGSTER'S SYN I II III

THE SAVAGE LIFE I II III

CHAINED TO THE STREETS

By J-Blunt

PUSH IT TO THE LIMIT

By **Bre' Hayes**

BLOOD OF A BOSS **I, II, III, IV, V**

SHADOWS OF THE GAME

By **Askari**

THE STREETS BLEED MURDER **I, II & III**

THE HEART OF A GANGSTA I II& III

By **Jerry Jackson**

CUM FOR ME I II III IV V

An **LDP Erotica Collaboration**

BRIDE OF A HUSTLA **I II & II**

THE FETTI GIRLS **I, II& III**

CORRUPTED BY A GANGSTA I, II III, IV

BLINDED BY HIS LOVE

THE PRICE YOU PAY FOR LOVE

By **Destiny Skai**

Ghost

WHEN A GOOD GIRL GOES BAD

By **Adrienne**

THE COST OF LOYALTY I II

By Kweli

A GANGSTER'S REVENGE **I II III & IV**

THE BOSS MAN'S DAUGHTERS I II III IV V

A SAVAGE LOVE **I & II**

BAE BELONGS TO ME I II

A HUSTLER'S DECEIT I, II, III

WHAT BAD BITCHES DO I, II, III

SOUL OF A MONSTER I II

KILL ZONE

By **Aryanna**

A KINGPIN'S AMBITON

A KINGPIN'S AMBITION **II**

I MURDER FOR THE DOUGH

By **Ambitious**

TRUE SAVAGE I II III IV V VI

DOPE BOY MAGIC I, II

MIDNIGHT CARTEL I II

By **Chris Green**

A DOPEBOY'S PRAYER

By **Eddie "Wolf" Lee**

THE KING CARTEL **I, II & III**

By **Frank Gresham**

THESE NIGGAS AIN'T LOYAL **I, II & III**

By **Nikki Tee**

GANGSTA SHYT **I II &III**

By **CATO**

THE ULTIMATE BETRAYAL

By **Phoenix**

BOSS'N UP **I , II & III**

By **Royal Nicole**

I LOVE YOU TO DEATH

By Destiny J

I RIDE FOR MY HITTA

I STILL RIDE FOR MY HITTA

By **Misty Holt**

LOVE & CHASIN' PAPER

By **Qay Crockett**

TO DIE IN VAIN

SINS OF A HUSTLA

By **ASAD**

BROOKLYN HUSTLAZ

By **Boogsy Morina**

BROOKLYN ON LOCK I & II

By **Sonovia**

GANGSTA CITY

By **Teddy Duke**

A DRUG KING AND HIS DIAMOND I & II III

A DOPEMAN'S RICHES

HER MAN, MINE'S TOO I, II

CASH MONEY HO'S

By Nicole Goosby

Ghost

TRAPHOUSE KING **I II & III**

KINGPIN KILLAZ I II III

STREET KINGS I II

PAID IN BLOOD **I II**

CARTEL KILLAZ I II III

By **Hood Rich**

LIPSTICK KILLAH **I, II, III**

CRIME OF PASSION I II & III

By **Mimi**

STEADY MOBBN' **I, II, III**

THE STREETS STAINED MY SOUL

By **Marcellus Allen**

WHO SHOT YA **I, II, III**

SON OF A DOPE FIEND

Renta

GORILLAZ IN THE BAY **I II III IV**

DE'KARI

TRIGGADALE I II

Elijah R. Freeman

GOD BLESS THE TRAPPERS I, II, III

THESE SCANDALOUS STREETS I, II, III

FEAR MY GANGSTA I, II, III

THESE STREETS DON'T LOVE NOBODY I, II

BURY ME A G I, II, III, IV, V

A GANGSTA'S EMPIRE I, II, III, IV

THE DOPEMAN'S BODYGAURD

Tranay Adams

174

THE STREETS ARE CALLING

Duquie Wilson

MARRIED TO A BOSS… I II III

By Destiny Skai & Chris Green

KINGZ OF THE GAME I II III IV

Playa Ray

SLAUGHTER GANG I II III

RUTHLESS HEART I II

By Willie Slaughter

THE HEART OF A SAVAGE

By Jibril Williams

FUK SHYT

By Blakk Diamond

DON'T F#CK WITH MY HEART I II

By Linnea

ADDICTED TO THE DRAMA I II III

By Jamila

YAYO I II

A SHOOTER'S AMBITION

By S. Allen

TRAP GOD

By Troublesome

FOREVER GANGSTA

By Adrian Dulan

TOE TAGZ I II

By Ah'Million

KINGPIN DREAMS

By Paper Boi Rari

CONFESSIONS OF A GANGSTA

By Nicholas Lock

I'M NOTHING WITHOUT HIS LOVE

By Monet Dragun

CAUGHT UP IN THE LIFE

By Robert Baptiste

NEW TO THE GAME

By **Malik D. Rice**

Life of a Savage

By **Romell Tukes**

LOYALTY AIN'T PROMISED

By Keith Williams

Quiet Money

By **Trai'Quan**

<u>BOOKS BY LDP'S CEO, CA$H</u>

<u>TRUST IN NO MAN</u>

<u>TRUST IN NO MAN 2</u>

<u>TRUST IN NO MAN 3</u>

<u>BONDED BY BLOOD</u>

<u>SHORTY GOT A THUG</u>

<u>THUGS CRY</u>

<u>THUGS CRY 2</u>

<u>THUGS CRY 3</u>

<u>TRUST NO BITCH</u>

<u>TRUST NO BITCH 2</u>

<u>TRUST NO BITCH 3</u>

<u>TIL MY CASKET DROPS</u>

<u>RESTRAINING ORDER</u>

<u>RESTRAINING ORDER 2</u>

<u>IN LOVE WITH A CONVICT</u>

<u>Coming Soon</u>

BONDED BY BLOOD 2

BOW DOWN TO MY GANGSTA

Ghost